a
drawn
&
papered
heart

Kallisto Gaia Press Inc.
1801 E. 51st Street
Suite 365-246
Austin TX 78723
info@kallistogaiapress.org
(254) 654-7205

Cover Design: Linda Konkoski
Cover layout: John Burger
Author Photo: Laura Alexander
Edited by Tony Burnett

ISBN: 978-1-952224-35-5

a
drawn
&
papered
heart

stories

Beth Konkoski

Table of Contents

The heart will break, but broken, live on.
   - Lord Byron

To my family, near and far: I am a writer partly because you have all believed in me and encouraged me over the years. I am forever grateful.

A Drawn and Papered Heart

It pays fifty bucks an hour, and the class is three and a half hours long. Not the sort of thing you tell your mother about, but we'll make rent. And it isn't as bad as I expected. I was nervous, but the first night, we stopped for dinner and after two beers and some enchiladas, I relaxed. I told Richard about the zit on my back. "Will they notice? Draw it?"

"It isn't about perfection," he said finishing his third Corona. Do colleges care about professors drinking before class?

Tonight, I slip out of my jeans and into the white robe I have carried over the mountain to this community college in the desert. Richard teaches Life Drawing 201 here at night after a day of high school art classes because they hire him, and college teaching looks good on his resume. But he complains. "Nobody down here willing to model. How do you teach a fucking life drawing class without a model?"

And that is where I fit in. The curtained space I stand in has art room props on a shelf behind me: dried flowers, a paper mache dog sculpture, a tarnished silver ice bucket, arms and legs from a mannequin. It is a small, thrown together changing room, the size of a shower, comforting the first night when I was so nervous about undressing, but now I feel a little foolish, hiding back here to transform from person to model. Why don't I just take off my clothes and leave them in a pile by the stool? I guess that would feel more intimate, letting my jeans slide off my thighs in front of the students, mostly young Mexican boys with perfect skin and hair that falls like rain when they take off their baseball caps. They are beautiful, each of them, but especially Antonio. I try to find poses that will keep me looking his direction, able to see the squinting, dense focus that crosses his

1

face when he draws me.

Before stepping on the wooden platform, I look around on the shelves for props to hold. Last week Richard went nuts when I wrapped my arms through an empty wooden picture frame, its gilded surface shedding gold paint on my shoulder.

"The angles, the angles," he proclaimed, making me shift at least five times with my body contorted inside the rectangle. I expected modeling to be dull, maybe some time to think a little about the three classes I still need to take for my Master's in Special Ed. so I don't lose my job. Then there's the visit from my parents to worry about; their attitude toward Luke has not improved since the wedding and they will require an especially well-planned story if I am to cover up his ill-fated military career and current job as a surfer of channels in our apartment. It isn't like I'm ok with where he's at; I'm just trying to have a little patience.

Anyway, the hours on this small stage aren't slow or empty at all. I realized the first night, hot under the lights and keeping my calves flexed while I crouched on the edge of the stool, that I am part of the finished product in an active sense. Somehow my energy shows up on their pages, and the drawings are always better when I focus on how I am positioned and who is drawing me. I have to push the pose out at them and think about it, watching the sweep of the second hand on the clock so I move on a schedule: eight poses at thirty seconds, six at two minutes, four at four minutes and two at six minutes. We run through this pattern then take a break. The second session begins with four minutes and moves to the final, almost impossible sixteen that feels like six hundred. When my mind drifts, Richard knows. When I walk around the easels on break and see what they draw, I can tell the poses that deflated or kept me too much in my head.

There is a vase tucked behind a pile of duck decoys, and I pull it toward me. The bottom scrapes like fingernails on the metal shelf and kicks up art dust, a mix of all their erasing and scribbling and sharpening. It smells of brush cleaner, chalk, and failure this dust that settles on my arms and travels deep into my lungs when I pose. The vase is large enough to hug and painted with metallic gold paint. I don't believe it has held flowers in this decade as it smells dry as a late summer creek.

A single rose sits across the stool. The outer petals curl like a lipsticked mouth, just a small pout off the head of the bloom. I touch its velvet, then lift it from the stool and look around. Antonio's eyes meet mine above his easel.

"For Valentine's," he says. And his gaze returns to the page even though he has nothing yet to sketch. A pulse kicks alive in my groin and at my collarbone, like I've been doing a quick set of jumping jacks. At the stool I cannot quite decide what to do with the rose or the vase, and the lights are small lasers on the back of my head, their heat traveling through my hair to spike me.

"We're ready?" Richard asks. The students step to their easels and face me. The rose and vase are an impossible match. The mouth would hold three dozen, so I place the single one on the floor and let my robe slip off as well. I balance on the stool with my legs out like a frog's, the vase hugged tightly against my breasts, my face turned so a cheek touches the rim. I stare at nothing on the classroom wall.

Antonio's rose has reminded me that I did not buy Luke a card for Valentine's Day, our second as a married couple. But he has been so difficult since his discharge, not even waking up when I leave for work, on the couch with Styrofoam takeout boxes beside him when I get home. He seems like a different person these last months and helping him feels both awkward and exhausting, especially since he barely answers my questions about the simplest things like getting the mail or buying a paper for want ads. "I hear you" is his preferred response, if he answers at all. So, the idea of romance has not been much on my mind, but still, six years together, two married and I blow it off. It is all I can think of for the thirty second poses, and this makes me hold them too long. Richard must cue me, cue me, cue me. The irritation is thick in his voice.

* * *

On the dining table when I was a child I would lay out all the Valentine cards in the box my mother purchased, trying to match the message of the card with the right person from class.

3

One year I couldn't decide on the card for Robbie Gleason who came up behind me on the playground and grabbed my elbows, pulled me to him and whispered, "Will you go out with me?" The only place to go in the fifth grade was the skating rink, so we spent the winter skating circles together after his hockey practice, my hand clenched in his through mittens so thick we could have been holding wooden sticks. As the rink shut down one Friday night, we skated a circle in the dark and he snow-plowed in the far corner, pulling me into the shadows where he pressed me against the wood, his cold lips like a flint the instant they touched mine. I can see myself at the table searching for the right card, getting annoyed as I shuffled and reshuffled, finally randomly putting them in envelopes and signing names on the front only. Nothing on those cards could tell him how his kiss made me think of summer and warm coals even as the wind blew against us. And I was scared to give him something noticeable, something from the drugstore in town that would state things clearly. On Valentine's Day he left a heart-shaped box of chocolates on my desk—To Shelly, From Robbie. The box was still in the closet of my old room; he had not been afraid.

* * *

"Michelle." The voice pulls at me, and I jerk myself off the stool. "Please." Richard's impatience and superiority are a vapor in the room. He points to the clock with his sharp, goateed chin, an artsy look he cannot pull off, and scolds me with the narrowing of his eyes. I am glad I turned down his suggestion that we sleep together after class the first night. At the time I felt a little bad about how harsh I sounded saying no, but he knows I'm married. More importantly, he is at least fifteen years older than me, and I don't think I hid that thought very well. His face sort of emptied and he mumbled, "Of course not," as he led us to his car. In the teacher's lounge at school the next day, he apologized without looking at me, but wanted to know if I would still model. "You're good, and I don't want to lose a model or be weird with a colleague," he said before walking away. I wondered how sleeping together would have left us "not weird," but it wasn't really worth going into. Luke wouldn't have liked me still riding over the mountain with him if he knew about the

4

proposition, but I am not in the habit of telling him everything I experience. I have assessed the risk and weighed the options; I'm pretty sure I can overpower Richard if he ever presses it, so I don't worry. I turn my focus to the clock and the angles of my body until break.

"I liked your shoulders in this one." Jose points, and I see the solid twist of torso, a neck long and looking away. They never draw more than an outline, a suggestion of me in space. Richard says they are learning how the body connects and doesn't, how different it looks from what they expect. I hear him telling a student that he wasn't looking carefully, didn't really see. Tightening the belt on my robe, I step away from the circle and into the hall. I will walk to the bathroom for something to do.

"You didn't look at mine tonight." His voice sounds like wings in the dark.

"Sorry." I step to where he leans against a bank of windows. Outside the sun has turned everything to some scrambled art tapestry of orange and vomit pink. The clouds look like crumpled laundry.

We are only a few feet apart, and I can see a pulse in his throat. His arms cross at his heart and he doesn't look away. He has been in my thoughts all night; if I'm honest, before tonight. I want to dig around in the space behind his eyes, to feel the shine of his hair across my skin.

"Thank you for the rose."

"You're welcome. He looks me in the eyes now. "Valentine's Day is for beauty." The classroom door opens, and we are both startled by Richard searching, spotting, scowling.

"Time," he says like a referee. Antonio hustles himself toward the call, so I am unable to say anything. I just follow, watch him move in his jeans and let his words repeat inside my head. For the second half of class I am anchored on the stage, imagining what Antonio will think of each pose, how he will shift me onto paper. Even the sixteen-minute ones feel short as I breathe my way around what I will say to him after class. At the end of the night there is never an inspection of work, just the hurry to be done and away. But if I dress quickly, I should be able to catch him in the parking lot while Richard closes up the room.

The night is almost chilly when I step outside. I can see a group of them walking together toward the scattered cars in the lot. Their voices sound as young as kids on a playground as they toss goodbyes around. I hurry to catch up. Antonio peels off toward a pick-up truck near one of the light posts. I am ready to call his name when the passenger door opens. High heels click on pavement.

"Antonio?" And then a spectacular girl in a leather mini dress emerges from behind the truck's cab. Her body flashes through the dark like a meteor in its confidence and layered gold. "It took so long," she says.

"Gloria." He steps toward her, kisses her with his arms cupping her chin. She wraps herself around him, into him, a little leap and her legs circle his waist. He boosts her higher on his hips and kisses her harder. They crash against the side of the truck, and I can hear them both moan. I am grateful for the dark and the moment of not calling his name. Back on the sidewalk, I drop Antonio's rose in the blue recycle container and pace quietly in the shadows, waiting for Richard who will drive us back over the mountain.

Desert Horse

On the afternoons I managed to escape my mother's house, I walked a six-mile loop around Lake Manor. On its shore crouched an abandoned playground, and the curving pavement turned without announcement into a country road of empty farmhouses. I call the farmhouses empty because I never saw anyone come in or go out, work on lawns or pull grocery bags from the yawning ends of station wagons, never, except in the case of the girl I am going to tell about. She has no name, at least not for me, and this lack is complete; I can imagine no name for her. She was a physical presence, an audience only. I am quite sure she was insane, or at least quite disturbed, for there was a certain pattern lost to the deep of her eyes and the grasping of her motile fingers. She emerged on the road utterly without story; yet I cannot convince myself this excuses what I did.

I wanted her for an audience, on this point I am clear. Perhaps it is important to know I have always wanted an audience. When I was a child the walls of my bedroom were decorated with several brown, metal-clasped envelopes holding pieces of my writing, short descriptive bits about my back lawn, the smell of the garden after tilling, new snow and the creek running beside our house when it filled to a level of threat with each spring thaw. Written on the front of the envelopes was a statement, "Read if you like," and at every opportunity, holiday, Sunday dinner, an evening with my mother's friends, I would drag guests up to my room and set them in motion. Like customers in a checkout line, they waited their turn by the stations, helpless once they agreed to enter.

I returned to live in the home of my childhood and travel around the lake as a thirty- seven-year old man, nurse to my nearly paralyzed mother during the day and wandering pro-

7

crastinator in my free hours. I set out for my walk as soon as the night nurse, a Miss Platinum, relieved me. The nurse is relatively unimportant; I mention her for authenticity and because she had a passionate, excessive hobby which she practiced while on duty. Miss Platinum was a prodigious crocheter; she made afghans for the Veteran's hospital in town, and each November her picture appeared in the paper, dwarfed beside two stacks of afghans or with one of her afghan recipients—a crumbled old man in a hospital bed. Over the years, she manufactured nearly three hundred afghans of scratchy, acrylic yarn, in a repeating V pattern called chevron. One rainy afternoon she produced a scrapbook to share with mother.

"I've been in the paper eighteen times," she told my mother with obvious pride. Such a level of productivity astounds me.

My cyclic, repetitive walks scoured away the hours of morning when I carried my mother's bedpans, brought weak Earl Grey tea she rarely could drink, and nodded off in the stuffy, book-lined living room between sneezes caused by my allergy to her cat, Moses, and the constant circulation of thick dust swirling in the light like a mini tornado whenever a door was opened or closed. Mother had a stroke during a spring ice storm that knocked down phone lines and kept her friends locked in their houses for two days. A neighbor noticed her paper on the step the afternoon of the storm and got help. The stroke left her unable to speak and barely able to scratch out cryptic messages on the stenographer's pad which remained posed beside her good right hand. As reduced as she was, however, she carried on the drama of her life in a tense narrative pattern of snoring. This snoring frightened me whenever I was in her room; for it rose to shrill catching wheezes of air and then ceased in a climax without breaths.

The first time I noticed this troubled story of air and lungs, I dropped the bed clothes I was carrying and rushed to her side to perform mouth to mouth resuscitation. Her face grew a deeper gray as I watched and listened for a breath. Finally, with a rush and huge intake, she snorted and her entire body jolted as if touched by a wet electrical cord. Her eyes flew open and then closed as she settled deeper onto her pillows and began the spiral again.

At the time of my mother's stroke, I had a sabbatical coming from the junior college where I teach anthropology. I have had a sabbatical coming for the last nine years as I try and change, begin and abandon various projects on which to base a Ph.D. dissertation. As I look back on it now, I had nothing of permanence to claim me in California. Stella, my wife and a photographer of some distinction, welcomed my departure. She felt the distance and space might push me over the hump, so to speak and actually get me writing the long-awaited thesis. Unfortunately, the season of nursing and solitude did not cure me; I never moved beyond the ardent piling and alphabetizing of my notes.

On the afternoon I finally spoke to the girl, I was tired from a difficult night with mother and confused by the photographs I received from my wife. I can see now how the photographs are linked to my moments with the young girl. It is obvious the horse connects them.

I parked myself on a swing by the lake, my rear end uncomfortable in the narrow canvas seat. Amidst the remains of November leaves drifting like brown rain, I reread Stella's letter. Her work was going well; her photographs had been written up in a Los Angeles magazine; she was busy each night in the darkroom and enclosed some prints to provide me with a sense of where her work was going. Fairly impersonal, certainly not a love letter, but such is and has always been, her style; my wife is nothing if not a businesswoman. When I finished the letter, I turned my attention to an aerial photograph of the horse. My horse, the horse I first went to see a few months before my mother's stroke. Not a real horse of flesh and blood, but a horse carved by ancient hands out of the desert floor. Its shape and construction still haunted my senses; its body riddled me with the mystery of its proportions. After visiting it, I did vast research into the Quechan people, most likely the creators of the horse, and once again, my dissertation swerved onto a new path.

Stella's photograph disappointed me. I sat with my legs cramped in the small space between the swing and ground, my

9

running shoes scraping dirt with each soft push of my body while I stared at her rendering of the horse- its outline from two hundred feet above the earth. Eventually I resumed my walk.

Don't think I have left the horse, dangled it before you to tease and now willfully eliminate it from my prose. The horse is elemental, the story, for it is what I would soon tell the young girl, the story she would listen to and somehow, misunderstand. Or did she get it too well, sense too much? It all wants to tumble out now, quickly and without structure.

Remember the horse and remember how Stella and I disagreed. As I moved in my familiar walking path, I realized the truth of the photos, the flattening, devoid sensation the horse caused when viewed from the air. She was wrong, wrong to try and capture its essence from above. Its artist could never have conceived of her viewpoint, could not have risen so high above his work, nor had reason to. This argument resounded in my head, gained momentum and convinced me my critical vision made sense. I sloped along, growing sure of an artistic victory over my more successful wife, the first victory in a long time.

The girl stood swaying on the edge of the pavement ahead of me; her boots clipped the highway when she rocked forward. I noticed the deep black of those boots, their weight and the bird-like thinness of the legs above them. I saw her on several other days, enough to feel she was almost part of the afternoon routine. With her Airedale on a nylon red leash, I always caught her somewhere along the gravel driveway that led back to a peeling white farmhouse, a dripping porch on the side packed with boxes, and in one window, an old rusted plow. She had chopped black hair, thick bangs and a round, monkey face. Her skittish, never ceasing eyes looked so small they nearly left the area between her forehead and nose. The first time I saw her, I took her for a boy with the boxy look of her red hunting jacket and the lumbering, awkward run into which she broke when I moved past her driveway.

As the days continued, she stopped running and I began to raise my hand and say hello, to which she coughed a tense greeting. I would not have called us friends, acquaintances even, but on that day she stood so close to the road as I approached, my left shoulder would have brushed her face if I had not moved out in a circle away from her. It was the nearest I had ever been, and I noticed her padded shape came from layers of clothes beneath the jacket. I could see a thick argyle sweater, at home on a ski slope, a maroon turtleneck and the collar of a denim shirt poking out below her ear. She held the dog's leash and I could hear snuffling among the leaves behind her.

"I made it to the road," she announced, the first words she ever spoke to me.

"You what?"

"I made it, look, I can even touch it," and she bent and placed her palm on the blacktop.

She claimed this so sincerely and with such pride I could think of nothing to say except, "Congratulations."

"Thanks," she returned, beaming some more. "I haven't been out this far since they brought me home in the summer."

The oddness of her statement made my spine tense, but I was curious. And all the sudden, I had to tell her about the horse. I didn't understand the damn thing myself, but she pulled the story from the back of my throat.

"You want to hear a story? About a horse in the desert." She didn't say anything right away, didn't even seem to hear me. Only her eyes moved, down to the toes of her boots and rested on the space where her driveway met the road.

"I've never seen a desert," she said finally when I was just ready to walk away, aware of my own foolishness. "I've never even seen a horse, not live and close up. A pony once at a game farm when I was small. I've never seen anything. I'll hear your story." She turned around and started down the driveway, "Come on," she waved me after her, and I followed. Of course, there was much implicit tension and danger in our meeting. However, most of it resided on her side; I was bigger, older, a man. I could have, but did not, rape her, seduce her, murder her. The newspapers are filled with such horrible deeds, and it makes encounters like ours unlikely, nearly impossible in our present world. But somehow her rules shifted, and she seemed completely without fear. On our trip down the driveway she stopped to point out boot marks in the mud.

11

"Every day I went one boot length further. Crazy huh? My parents freaked when the school called and told them to come get me. Hadn't left my room for three weeks. Nutty." She shook her head and the bangs flapped against her forehead like small waves.

"I just didn't believe it was out there. You know? But you've seen a lot, traveled. Well, I'm getting better. The floor kissing my feet and all that."

There seemed no fitting response, so I remained silent, and continued to follow her moving, woolen back. We soon reached the house where she pulled open a battered screen door and scooted past the stairs onto the porch. With the door's creak, the dog bounded from the woods, pushing me out of the way as he licked and wiggled around her. I followed them both onto the porch, but halted when the smell of the place struck my nose. I have never smelled anything so old and rotting, like flower stems left stinking in their vase water. The porch was a large rectangle, three sides windowed, but piled almost six feet high with crates and garbage bags, so the only light came from over my head in thin wisps through the thick paned and bubbled glass. A wood stove stood throwing warmth in the far corner of the room and a dilapidated old couch, hideous yellow and green plaid, sat dangerously close to the heated metal.

"Have a seat," she motioned me to the ugly, dog hair-covered sofa. I hesitated, fumbled with my original desire to talk to her.

"Want some hot chocolate?" She began peeling layers of clothing, thinning herself like an onion. Her final, small frame made me wonder how old she was; she mentioned school, college-maybe eighteen? I realized we were going no further into the house when she got a pan from a nail on the wall and leaned down amid one of her massive stacks. I heard the rubber pull of a refrigerator door, and she straightened with a quart of chocolate milk in her hand. She poured the frothing brown liquid into the pan and set it on the wood stove's flat top.

"You stay on the porch?"

"My daytime spot; I hear anyone coming and wait for my parents. They don't get home until after dark."

A few moments later I took the thick mug she handed me and rested back against the cushions, springy and surprisingly comfortable. The horrible smell of the place faded as I relaxed and seemed more like freshly turned dirt after a spring rain. My hostess folded her gangling, thin legs and settled like a graceless ostrich on the carpet before the wood stove. I leaned further back, lost the sense of where I was. Perhaps it was only the release of so many tense weeks; I am generally inclined not to believe in the more mystical possibilities; but I felt removed from my situation even as I consciously gripped the hot mug and felt the prickle of dog hair through my shirt. Altered, switched in time, too much like my first horse experience.

"This horse," she nudged in a soft, ethereal voice like the rub of a cotton ball on my cheek.

"I've wanted to tell about it for a long time. My wife doesn't believe what happened, won't or can't acknowledge what may have been out there. I thought of trying to write about it, an essay or something, then my dissertation."

"I'll believe you. Really." This made me sit up and look.

"You see a lot when you stay in one room for three weeks."

"We piled out of the back of a pick up after fifteen miles of washboard. Stella knew where we were. I was lost, unsure as always of direction in the depth of the desert. Even the sun was no help, beating down, filling the air rather than moving in a direction or existing as its usual sky disc self. There was only the atmosphere of heat out there, bright, oppressive and spread without shape or direction."

"What does a desert smell like?"

"Smell like?" I had to open my eyes again when she spoke, but closed them to think of an answer. My nostrils pulled, "Dry. Sand covered wood, like the first moments of a campfire." I saw her nose twitch too, heard her draw a deep breath.

"Ok."

Our guide to the horse was a twenty-five-year desert explorer and amateur archaeologist, Craig Sadwick. With him was his much younger girlfriend, Rosie and her three sons, all blonde and bouncing. They disappeared after a jackrabbit a few minutes after we arrived. I didn't know precisely where we were, but I could locate Mexico only a quarter mile away across the All American Canal. Green, lushly watered fields, placed artificially in the desert through a series of government funded irrigation projects and the music of a rodeo or carnival gave the other side of the canal a livelier and far more cared for look than the baked desert hills on which I stood. Craig told us the area was closed at night, "The damn wetbacks. I find their clothes floating some mornings in plastic garbage bags."

"Where do they go?"

"Go?"

"The people who float their clothes?"

"Oh," I considered a moment, "They try to get to Los Angeles or San Diego, Riverside or El Centro if the harvest is on." She didn't look exactly sure.

"Did you see any?"

"No. And they're not part of the story." She allowed me to continue.

As we headed up into the higher hills, he told us to stay off anything beaten down like a path or trail. Most of the area is still unmarked, unclaimed, archaeological territory. I watched the ground for the places not to walk and became enraptured by the rocks- shiny, black, covered with desert varnish and baked into the earth like a cobblestone road. Along the way, Craig pointed out three separate sleeping circles, clear, hard-pressed sand, free of all but the tiniest pebbles. Artifacts are everywhere down there, hammer stones, grinding stones, every kind of implement or rock tool. If we wanted to hold an object for a closer look, we were instructed to mark its spot with a piece of grass or other stone before removing it from the ground. In truth, each item had to be pried from the earth and left its own shape, cast in the hard desert soil. Mostly I left things alone; their invisible, mosaic felt deeper than my need to touch.

We passed from all black pebbles to areas with peach, almond and copper stones, many ringed with the black, striped bands of desert varnish around their circumference. Craig paused again at a quartz reduction circle, a religious spot where the Quechan beat quartz crystals with a hammer stone to release power. He showed us an actual hammer stone, an undeniable handle worn away by human sweat and toil; then he pointed to the winking crystals covering a rough circle pounded into the ground. When a crystal broke, the Quechan took the released energy into their bodies and spirits.

"How does it happen?"

"What?"

"The power. How does it get into them?" I looked at her again, annoyed by her interruptions. I didn't know how it was supposed to happen. All my research on the Quechan had not told me; even worse, I hadn't thought to wonder. She unfoldied while I talked and with her legs out before her, she picked at the carpet with long fingers, pulling up lint and stray wood chips.

"It's different for each of them," I lied, "but through the chest mostly, near the heart I think." She didn't answer, just gazed at me and briefly rubbed a hand across her chest. I began again.

We crested a hill and there was the horse, about half the size of a football field, an outlined monument of stones. The possibility of its creation did not strike me at once; in fact, my first reaction was a letdown. I imagined it much differently, expected a pile of stones or a sculpture rising out of the desert floor. Instead it rested in flowing form on the ground, its shape a negation of space, a clearing out. It might be called a crude representation upon first encounter; Stella's aerial photographs capture it as such, and I recall she immediately began snapping her shutter from all angles, waxing about its proportions, its precision. I simply walked in circles, humbly keeping a wide berth, seeing him from all angles.

It did not immediately awe or render breathless; it did not shock; merely existed, and as I traveled in my circles and blocked out the noise of the camera, I began to notice how he changed his sense of motion as I altered my location. At times he leaps, and from other positions he is still and watching. Rocks edged up high along the front flank and the tail gives the body depth and shimmer. The surface, internal sense of his body is pushed free of the desert varnished rocks and the outline emerges from this clearing, this pushing back of the baked cobblestones. He looks like a clean swept floor, slightly dug and rounded into the earth.

"Did he have a saddle? The pony I saw had this old leather thing and a dirty wool blanket."

"No, no saddle. A wild horse."

"Wild, yes, wild," she intoned back to me, and I noticed she started to rock slightly, toward her outstretched toes and back again.

From the north end view, my feet somewhere below his stomach, his neck stretches far out; the sense of motion, of weight above the artist's imagined plane, is distinct. He runs, gallops, lopes, lengthens toward the south east, toward the water and Mexico.

When I stood above him, several feet from the base of his tail, he moved upright, straight and waiting. I reveled in this illusion for many circles, watching and proving the consistency of the trick. Stella had reached her judgement by this time, "Beautifully primitive and worthy of an aerial shot." Immediately she wandered off to see if Craig knew a pilot. I stood alone with the horse. Our guide had dated it at approximately three hundred years old. I wondered about its purpose, why face it to the southeast, what did it look for, wait for? Did the artist hope to call horses to him and the tribe?

Horse. I said the word several times, wondering about the name the artist would have had for his perfectly rendered animal. The Quechan people would not have had horses when this one was fashioned on the desert floor. But the Spaniards may have passed by, materializing like Gods on huge, magical beasts. Over these thoughts, I first heard the noise. It seemed like the wind or a discordant note from across the canal, someone scraping a bow across one fiddle string. I turned to look for the noise and when I looked back around, I was blinded by the hot, low west of the sun. The rhythmic humming continued and as my eyes grew used to the sun, I saw a hunched figure, squatting near the horse's rear flank. He brushed his hands over the smooth, clear dirt, eased some heavy dust to the line separating the two back legs, then surveyed his work and straightened.

"Could you see through him, like a ghost?" This time I

16

was angry."

"Shut up. This is the most important part," I looked at her with a glare to keep her quiet. She wasn't sitting anymore; instead she had curled over her knees in an embryonic squat and rocked on her toes.

"Are you ok?"

"Yes. Sorry. Please go on." She said all this in a muffled way, the words coming through lips pressed to her leggings.

When he stepped back from his horse he appeared slightly above five feet tall with knotted muscles along his thighs and shoulders. While I watched, he raised his hands to the sky and the low, intoned moaning grew louder, its intense, meditative hum settling on the wind. The figure turned and faced me while lowering his arms and looked exactly where his horse looked. I felt as if he saw me, but could not be sure. His gaze chilled and then elated as he raised his arms once more to the sky and smiled. I can't recall what he wore, but as his smile reached its zenith, I saw a perfect row of teeth. He stood in this mantra position only a moment longer and then snapped his arms to the side, stepped with one foot toward me and thrust his arms forward as if throwing a large, heavy object. I jumped when he did this, startled enough to blink for a second and he was gone when I looked again.

That is basically how I remember telling my story. I didn't tell her how the encounter shook me. I had never even admitted to Stella his occasional appearance in my dreams, the look in his eyes as he gazed east haunting me with its artistic desire and mystery. The arm snap, so full of command even in its possible futility, mocked my own slovenly efforts at control of any kind; he believed in his power to send the figure off, to call horses to him from the intensity of his wanting.

When I finished, I sat up completely, still holding the now cold cup of cocoa and looked at her. Have I made it sufficiently clear her awkward and confusing demeanor? Do you see her as I did, tripping down the driveway all gangling legs and fear? I hope so, or this next makes little sense. As I turned to gaze on her, I observed her change of position during the last part of my story. Now she crouched on the floor of the porch, but not wrapped around herself, instead, open and moving with a rush and a gesture.

She squatted; I looked at her and recognized something from earlier, from my mind, my own story. Of course, it is difficult to recreate the split second I realized what I was watching, the squat, the replication. She was on the rug, leaning over something in the exact position of my desert apparition. Her body had even taken on his muscled lines; I actually saw her thigh ripple under her tights. They were the same. And then she turned and looked at me; she brushed her hand in a tracing line, a delicate, curving function of a line, lovingly, ingeniously rendered and stood up.

"Isn't it perfect, just perfect?" she looked me full in the face and the gray of her eyes had hollowed, tunneled away from the present. In those eyes, their light, their contained, licking fire, rested the energy I had glimpsed in the desert.

"Sure," it seemed the only thing to say.

"Thank you. So much" and she sighed deeply while bending once more to something she saw on the floor. I know what she believed; I had given her the materials. One version of this story suggests I simply tiptoe from the porch and leave her with the joys and problems of her creation. A sufficient denouement had been achieved-- communication, transfer of sensation. Why did I not revel and go home? Ah the web I've spun; I squirm under its responsibilities, but against my will I must continue, on to the bitter end, even though you will think less of me when you hear what I did. But why couldn't I leave her? Wasn't she where I would have her? She had shown me my story, my horse; proven me right beyond a doubt.

See her as in a kind of trance, sweeping and pawing at the floor. My narrative, mine had placed her there! But she was beyond my story too, and I writhed with jealousy as her ownership struck me with the hollow gong of unpleasant truth. Regrets now are of little importance. I believe I did pause, the tiniest doubt at destroying this moment I had created. But I apply that word now, after the fact; I'm sure I didn't think it then.

"I never told you why they haven't catalogued all the artifacts." I can still hear the oily lean in my voice. "There are others like it all over Anza Borrega; but when they mark them and put up fences to protect them, people come to destroy. They bust through the signs and ride four wheelers around because they hate the fences keeping them out. They want free land for their circles and races. Hundreds of miles to tear across and they resent several acres of wire fence protecting the past." She still squatted in perfect, graceful imitation, confident as she brushed and arranged like a child play cooking.

"It already happened to the horse," she tensed at this, had really been listening all along. "Some kids came along with spray paint and wrote 'fuck you" just above its back, all white rocks."

She rose slowly as I told her this; her eyes no longer tunneled but filled with the cold flicker of insanity's anger.

"Take that back," through clenched teeth, a snaking, whistle of a voice.

"Take it back or I'll kill you." She did not fly at me or lose control; if she had I would have laughed and shook it off as senseless passion. Instead she stood there, rising and somber, her eyes a crystal of intent.

"I'm not joking," she said again in the hushed tone of an angry mother in church. I found myself edging toward the door, backing as though from a snarling dog. Then in an instant of pure motion, she attacked with clawed fingers and a taloned, unrecognizable face. I tripped on a box, fell onto my back and rolled from beneath her fighting body. I made it off the porch somehow and ran the three miles to my mother's house without looking behind me, forcing the pitch of her final screams out of my head as thoroughly as I could.

And that, with an action climax is what happened, what finished my stay with the girl, for I never dared to walk the loop again. I drove by in the early morning once and saw no sign of anyone; the house looked as sagging and desolate as ever. My mother died several months afterward, and I left for California near the end of winter, my dissertation as abysmally nonexistent as when I had arrived. Stella decided she needed a break from what she called the "rigors of marriage," whatever the hell that means. She has taken an apartment in Los Angeles and continues to send me notices of her work and proofs on which to comment. She claims to still enjoy my "critical eye" even though I find her work to be empty and paper doll-like, lacking in the life I thought she once displayed; of course, my opinion might be slightly bitter.

Though I did not see the girl again, her image has lingered and mixes continually with my thoughts of the horse. I hope I did not harm her; it seems a distinct possibility. But my jealousy lingers as well, an unpleasant, greasy longing. For I want what she had in those brief moments on the floor of her porch. It will not come to me despite frequent visits to the horse and the continual hope for the figure that began it all. I long to know if his wish was answered in his lifetime, if he knows his creation has lasted, is occasionally threatened and brings joy to its infrequent visitors. The horse sits, day and night on a swell of desert land, a work of art more than three hundred years old.

Sonny Boy

My father's cousin, Bobby Burger, came home from Vietnam with a purple heart and black lungs. At least that's what he told my dad each time he stopped by to see him.

"Sonny Boy. I'm back and thirsty," he'd roar through the screen door at least twice a summer. I never understood why they called each other that name; Dad said it was just something that started when they were kids.

His laugh settled like a morning fog around our dining room table where he chain-smoked and drank cans of Schlitz almost as fast as I could fetch them. When he showed up, Dad turned off the radio, stopped puttering in the garage or mowing the lawn so he and Bobby could retell their stories of every fish they ever caught, every cast they ever made, every cow pasture, electric fence or posted sign that ever crossed their paths around St. Lawrence County when they were "young enough to think fun was a job."

"He's lucky to be alive." Dad told Mom when she complained about the length of his visits, how drunk he got. Six men went into a fox hole and only he came out. This was the heart of the story, the heroic waiting he did with five of his fellow soldiers dead around him, their bodies first bloating, then stinking as three days went by. "Can you even imagine an hour with a corpse on top of you, in the dark and not sure what's above ground if you claw your way out?" Mom didn't answer. "If shooting the shit helps him a few times a year, how can I say no?"

He didn't raise his voice to her often, taught me to speak with softness in the presence of a lady and to remember, "every girl's a lady." But on the subject of Bobby's visits, he would not give in. There was a place at our table and a case of

Schlitz for Bobby whenever he parked in our driveway, until the day he pulled the gun.

I remember a row of empty cans on the table, each one smashed against his forehead when he finished and then piled where we could see. He started to sweat about four beers in, and he looked slick as I stood beside him with another full can, his ninth. When his arm shot out and grabbed me around the neck, I was surprised. Close and tucked in by his armpit, he smelled of wet ashes and dirty sheets. Before I had time to gag, he pulled my chin upward forcing me to look in his eyes. At the same time, Dad yelled. "Sonny what the fuck?"

"You think I'm a hero?" His lips were only inches from my face. My head couldn't move in his grasp, and my mouth couldn't form any words. I heard the hollow metal certainty of a gun, cocked and then placed between my eyes. The cold seared its stillness into my skin. "Do you?" The icy spot on my forehead held my focus. When I shifted my eyeballs up in their sockets, a length of black seemed to grow like a horn, outward and endless. And then Bobby's face, spitting lips, eyes pulsing at me as the gun began to shake against my skin.

I never got the chance to answer. In the next moment, an explosion of movement on my right side and Bobby grunted as my dad threw his body into him. Together they toppled over and away from me. I heard the blast, previously only known to me outdoors, filling the room with a thick echo. My mom was beside me, dragging me by the shoulders, my feet scrambling as she pulled, her screams cutting through the remnants of the shot. She had me on the back porch and then the lawn before I ever got fully upright.

"Don't you move." Her look, like the story of the Greek woman who turned people to stone with her snake hair, froze me where I stood, even though I wanted to know what happened to Dad. She called to him through the screen, and the door squeaked into the now silent house. I could picture her crossing the linoleum, passing the kitchen table, pushing her way into the dining room. It seemed like hours before she came back, alone.

"Everything's fine Mrs. Atwell," she called, raising her

hand to our nearest neighbor. I hadn't even realized the old lady was on her back porch looking our direction. Then Mom's arms were around me and for the second time in less than twenty minutes, I was pulled tight against the body of an adult. This time I pushed away.

"Dad?"

"He's fine. The shot went through the wall and out the living room window. He's got Bobby tied up in an extension cord. He wants you to head over to Mark's house." She was a few feet away from me, her hands still reaching and twisting like she wanted to be holding onto me again.

"I'm not leaving." As the words came out of my mouth, I couldn't believe them. Apparently, a gun to the forehead freed me to talk back to my mom. Her hands found their proper job then, shaking me by the shoulders for such boldness.

"You will go because I told you to go. You will go because your father said to go. NOW!" And she turned me with the same violence that dragged me from the dining room only a few crazy minutes before.

So, I started across the back lawns, four houses until my best friend Mark's. But at Mrs. Atwell's garden, I stopped and looked behind me. Mom was inside. I creaked open our front door moments later, needing a look at this man who almost killed me. A siren howled a few streets away and for the first time in my life, I knew where it was going. High up on the front picture window, I saw a hole and thin spider lines in the glass. A swinging door separated our dining room from the front of our narrow house, all laid out in a line. I could hear quiet movement, like feet in soft slippers and once, a loud sigh. The siren was getting closer, so my time was nearly up. I crept to the edge of the couch, my hand on the door frame, my eye pressed to the thin crack of light between the door and the wood that surrounded it. I pushed just a little and a pair of legs came into view. Just as I worked up the courage to push it wider, a body appeared, and I fell forward into open space as my dad pulled the door from the other side.

I landed on Bobby's back, his tied-up body breaking my fall, and I scrambled off him like he was the boiling oil my mother cooked donuts in each fall, scalding and deadly, unlike anything I ever knew. But once I got myself backed into the corner of the dining room away from him, I let myself look and there was only Bobby, a sad version of him with his hands pulled behind his back, his slick body splayed across the floor and his eyes filled with tears. The drumbeats of my heart still pounding, I wondered where the gun had gone when Dad bound him in the cord. He looked like a trussed deer more than anything, harmless now. Snot ran out of his nose and across his lips, dripping onto the floor as he laid there, unable to wipe it away. I immediately longed to give him a handkerchief, and I stood up to go to my dresser and find one, but Dad glared at me, pointed with clear direction for me to stay where I was. His eyes let me know he would deal with me later, and it wouldn't be pleasant.

"Come on Sonny," he said, bending over to grab Bobby by an arm and help him to his feet. "Let's get you out of here and home." It was the voice he used to tell me where to cast my pole when we sat in our boat by the walleye hole, how to steady the shotgun as ducks appeared above us in the blind, how to find the lowest common denominator in my fractions homework: a gentle voice, slow and easy that let me know I could take all the time I needed to get things right. And here he was, sharing that voice with Bobby, only minutes after tackling him to the floor. The feel of metal on my forehead would not leave my mind, nor my mother's frantic hold on me, but I also wanted to wipe Bobby's nose, to ease him like Dad's hand on his elbow. He pulled the dining room door open again to guide them through and into our living room where they faced Mr. Hartney, the town cop, his pistol drawn and steady at Bobby's chest.

"It's ok Paul," Dad said, "We're gonna come on out to your car without any need for that gun." And Bobby just shuffled along beside him, never looking up or trying to pull away. They moved like the Siamese twins from the circus, through the living room and out the screen door onto our porch. In our driveway, Bobby's old Chevy pick-up with the crushed-in driver's door sat behind our station wagon; it would stay on our property for six months, and then disappear one night while I slept. After Dad helped Bobby lower into the back of the police car, guiding his head and then leaning in with a hand on his shoulder, he walked over to the truck and reached through the open window to pull out the keys. Without the siren drawing attention to itself, Mr. Hartney drove off down our street, the dark shadow of Bobby's head rocking in the back. I heard the keys rattle in the pocket of Dad's pants as he pulled me into his arms on the sidewalk. We stood in a hug even tighter than Bobby's grip had been, a fierce holding I did not want to end.

Golden Rule

The first time Francis McCandry destroyed the devil's ornaments in her neighborhood, she vomited at her backdoor before extinguishing her flashlight, scraping the mud from her shoes and sneaking through the dark maze of her kitchen. Upstairs, she slid beneath the blankets, settling into the warm cave made by her husband's shoulders. The next night she sneaked as carefully, worked more thoroughly crushing the cheap orange and white baubles and felt pride instead of nausea when she reached the cinderblock steps of home. On her third excursion, the voice took over, the voice of a demanding, venomous God, a cross between Neil Diamond and Pat Buchanan, exhorting her to "get on with it already" when she merely paused to wait for a passing car. But the voice wasn't really angry, just rushed; she recognized its tone, its mindset so like hers, frustrated with how far things had gone.

This year six houses on her block alone put up pumpkin and ghost lights, ten other houses had at least some form of ghoul hanging in a window or dangling by a hangman's noose from the trees in the front yard. It drove her just a little mad, watching it day after October day, this calling and cavorting with Halloween spirits, this demonstration of darkness. She was a quiet, well-mannered woman in her mid-sixties who drove to Washington each spring for the anti-abortion rally, said her rosary twice a day and attended mass unless the weather was absolutely impassable. She loved her neighbors despite their faults and tried to leave judgment to the Lord. Oh, there was much she could say about each of them, but she did the best she could to "treat others" and ignore the rest.

And so her life would have gone, these minor forays into enemy territory to revoke the satan worship she knew went on. The golden rule would have kept her in check had the Parows, in the house next door, not decided to desecrate their bathtub shrine where Mary, the Blessed Virgin, stood guard. Every Christmas for seventeen years, Walter Parow removed the Blessed Virgin in early December and placed the Holy Family inside. But this year, on October 1st, Francis stood with her dining room sheers around her like cobwebs, shocked and infuriated as Walter made a collage of Halloween gadgets, the centerpiece a witch and her green flashing cauldron all arranged like an evil mockery of the Holy Family. She did not sleep for three nights. By the fourth night, she recognized her mission, the necessity of reclaiming just a little of the church's power and dignity. This sin against the Virgin called for more than removal; retribution was now required. "Sometimes," the voice guided her toward her garage, "one must break a rule to teach others a lesson." Nodding her head in agreement, she found the gas can and her husband's blow torch. The Parows would know a reckoning.

Strawberries for Sale

When she got married, Carol said "for better or worse" like everybody else, and she certainly never imagined she would one day consider choosing between her husband and the space to plant a garden. They were visiting her parents for the Fourth of July, a big celebration in the town where she grew up. She had reached the point in her pregnancy when sleep was more disturbed than restful. As tired as she felt, the double bed in the guest room offered no comfort, particularly not with Rob snoring by her side. The rasping of the fan seemed to swell in her skull as the light evolved from tar to granite to butter near sunrise. She kicked the sheet off and hoisted herself upright. It was difficult to get used to the slow pace of her last trimester, the conscious effort all basic movement now required.

Her eyes drooped, her body swayed, still close to sleep as she stood in front of the coffee maker. None of her sister's children, also visiting for the Fourth of July weekend, had begun to stir yet. Even her father, normally puttering about in his to-mato plants by the first hint of day, was still in bed. She squinted at the clock over the stove, 6:38. Too damn early. The day would be endless, like the summer was endless as she waited, kept still and waited for their son to be born.

* * *

The sonogram at twenty weeks did not initially reveal the sex, and the doctor tried to steer their thoughts to other topics, the developing lungs, the presence of all internal organs. The beating heart got her attention, brought the baby to life when she could see the rhythm, the fast, breathy pace she sensed within. Their two pulses ran separately, but connected, and this little machine, almost the size of a marble, kept their fluids mingling.

"How about the sex doctor? That's what we really want to know." For a moment she hadn't recognized Rob's voice, so

pushy, while the hand on her shoulder tightened like a tourni-
quet until she felt trapped beneath the weight of his demand.
"Can you tell or not?" There was the lawyer, the other Rob who
left for work in his suit and BMW. They often joked about the
benefits of his forty-minute commute. "Time for my transfor-
mation." He would laugh and she would return. "The scary Dr.
Jekyll comes home to his wife." But Lawyer Jekyll spoke that
day and her wonderful, teddy bear doctor who always offered
his hand to pull her up from the table and patted her on the
knee before she left, sounded irritated as he looked again at the
images and clicked the buttons to section their baby into parts.
"What if he's wrong and it's a girl?" She asked him in the car
a few minutes after the appointment. She stared at the strip of
pictures, sorting the images that looked anything but human
now without the doctor's pointing and explanations.

"He's not wrong."

"But what if he is? It happens."

"He isn't. Do you think he would have said if he wasn't
sure?"

"Would a girl be so bad?"

"It's not a girl." Horns blared behind them as Rob
swerved the car into a tight niche in the outside lane. They never finished the conversation. He had his answer, and she knew
enough not to keep going once his mind was made up. Soon
the toy trains and race car sets began coming home. Their unborn child's closet filled steadily with toys unusable for at least
two years. And their weekends were a haze of blue shopping:
wallpaper, sheets, airplane lamps and mobile. He liked to read to
the baby while Carol sat with her feet elevated after dinner. *The
Little Engine that Could* was his favorite and leaning into her stomach he would sing "Take Me Out to the Ballgame," tapping out
the "1, 2, 3 strikes you're out" line just below her belly button.

"You think your parents thought about this as much as
we do?" He asked one night as he closed *The Cat in the Hat* and
kissed her where a foot or a knee just made a passing ripple.

"I was the fourth out of five. How could they have had
time?"

"I guess. Only two for my parents, but Dad always

29

worked midnights." He paused as the movement of her stomach began again, "I'll say no to a few cases next year. Adjust a little, you know." That was the night they finally eliminated Daniel from the list and agreed on Jackson, although Carol still secretly weighed the sound of Katherine and Vanessa when she was alone.

* * *

The touch on her shoulder made her jump. "You're up early," he whispered in her ear. His hand tracked down, across her swollen breasts and onto the rising hill of abdomen.

"How's the boy?"

"Baby! Can you call it a baby, just once?" The spoon she had been using to stir her coffee clattered to the floor as she pushed away from the countertop with both hands, bouncing her body against his and then moving away from him. Feeling behind and beneath to lower her weight, she sat heavily in a kitchen chair, then slumped and looked onto her parents' backyard. Their garden- weed free and immaculate, the corn not quite a foot high in yardstick-straight rows, beans, squash and cucumbers all emerging from the earth to blossom, bear fruit and become seeds again. She could feel Rob's eyes on her, waiting, and she tried to sink deeper in the study of the garden. Her childhood summers were filled with weeding, picking, chopping, freezing from a garden planted to feed seven. She hated it, she thought. And when she and Rob had been house hunting, it never occurred to her to look for room on which to grow things.

Tears worked slowly from the corners of her eyes and dropped, almost cool, on her cheeks. She pictured their house with no lawn, their upscale, can't hang a clothesline development and thought of it for the first time as empty instead of neat; it denied her things she thought she didn't want.

"What's wrong?" He was at her side. "I'll say baby, ok? Baby, baby, baby."

"Forget it. You know, it's just…" But she sobbed instead and couldn't finish. With her head on her arms she looked into brown, filtery light as tears dropped onto the kitchen table.

"Hormones. Don't worry; I get it."

"No!" She hated this argument he threw out to cover all

unusual behavior or requests. "It's not that. It's…"

"You're getting close. I see. No problem. You're forgiven. Just rest that son, I mean baby. Go back to bed? Sleep late?"

He really did worry about her, wanted what was best for both of them. She would never make her point without more exhausting tears, more emotion. And it might not ever be explained, the hopeless vision of their supposed dream home suddenly hovering in her mind.

"No. I'm ok." She picked her head up. "I'll just finish my coffee and walk."

"I was gonna run. But I'll go with you instead."

"Really?"

"Sure."

"Why? You never walk."

"I'm on vacation. I can run later. And I want to see you smile. You haven't much since we got here."

* * *

Thirty minutes later they were on Clear Pond Road, beneath a tent of trees and jagged sunrays passing through with the wind. Carol grew up biking and jogging around Clear Pond. The five-mile loop from her parents' home passed quickly from a residential neighborhood to farmland hugging the water's edge and rolling backward in acres of green, most of it planted in cow corn or hay to feed small herds of dairy cattle. These were small family farms, mostly run down, every house and barn needing shutters, paint, a new roof. Beneath the surface, rocky glacial soil, a hard living for anyone who tried to exist off this land. They both grew up in small farm communities, hours apart, but the mentality, the struggle was familiar from birth.

Rob hated the farms, their smells and their disheveled, downtrodden appearance. Carol ceased to notice them as a teenager, but now found them beautiful and stark. She lived away from this town for eight years, college and then the suburbs where she always dreamed she would go. Unexpectedly, she missed the space, the peace, the angry dogs running down dusty driveways, the tractors rusting into the ground. She noticed small details here, a giant fuchsia blooming on the only standing post of a front porch, a red checked apron shifting like a pennant from a clothesline.

"By definition a walk requires movement." At the sound of his voice she turned her eyes from the bushes where she was sure she saw a flash of blue.

"I think I saw a bluebird."

"You what?" He was a few yards ahead, his feet still on the pavement and facing away, his hands impatient on his hips. She hadn't taken a step yet to rejoin him.

"A bluebird. They're the state bird, but really rare around here. My dad and I used to put up houses for them, but we never got one to nest."

"Jesus Christ. Is this National Geographic? Today already." And he started down the road.

She caught up to him quickly and they walked until the lake lapped beside them, quiet without the waves of jet skis or powerboats the afternoon would bring. They stepped in unison around an explosion of broken glass, scattered around a paper bag and the strong smell of beer.

On a narrow strip of land between road and lake they reached a patch of wild lilies. Bright orange, their throats open to the sun, they spilled along, hundreds of them, and drifted into the trees. Carol stepped down from the road to walk among the flowers. The patch rose on a small hill so they nearly hid her until she climbed thoroughly among them. She let her fingers out, softly running along the velvety petals, the gentle sandpaper scratch of their thick, gossiping leaves. Bees buzzed in steady cadence, and she too longed to tunnel into a lily's orange and drink at the puddle of its nectar.

"What the hell are you doing?" He had not noticed when she stepped off the pavement this time and continued along, looking down the road and talking for nearly ten steps before realizing her absence. Her eyes closed, her head thrown back, her fingers moved as if she were playing a piano but touching only the flowers around her.

"Carol?" She heard him, but not loudly through the bees and the whispering of the petals she touched so intimately.

"Hey!" His voice closer, he grabbed her arm as he yelled for attention, spinning her sharply from the shoulder. She opened her eyes and looked at him, startled by the sudden whirling of her body and the anger in his eyes like a current shooting to ground through his grip.

"Let go of me!" For the second time that day she found his touch corrosive, impossible.

"Well what the fuck were you doing?"

And what could she say? Feeling the flowers, touching them? "Giving them to the baby." The idea came out of her mouth before she knew she had spoken, before thought even made her meaning clear. But it was what she meant, exactly.

"Bullshit!" He turned and started away, leaving his opinion to hang between them.

She wanted to scream back at him, ask why it was bullshit, why he had to be so rational, so like himself about everything. Her fists knotted and tight against her side, anger coiled within. But then tears instead, always tears. And what had she been doing really? How could she give flowers to an unborn child? Rob was nearly around the corner now, and she hustled to catch up to him, wiping her eyes on the way. As her fingers passed her nose, she could smell the dusty pollen and deep sunny odor of the lily patch; she rubbed her stomach as she stepped in line with Rob to continue their walk. She could hope.

It took a few hundred yards before he began speaking to her again, and they rounded the lake, moved up Madison Hill near an old gravesite where a few slowly weathering headstones and a rusted fence paid tribute to the once dominant, wealthy Madison family. Their farmland stretched for miles, but by the late 1950's, milk prices dropped, Madison children found other interests and the farm was left with nobody to keep it moving and breathing into the future. The main house still stood at the top of the hill, but it was a rental farm now; while the rest of the acres were sold off in portions. When Carol was young the house possessed a certain dignity, looking down onto the lake and over the rolling hills, but it was not cared for through the years, and by the time she graduated from high school, it lost parts of its roof and many windows, the driveway now a weedy lane of cracked pavement. It even stood empty for a few years and kids from school, more daring than she, reportedly used it as a place to drink and get wild.

But as they worked their way up the hill, it was clear the house had occupants. Two little girls stood by a card table set almost on the pavement.

"Wanna buy some strawberries?" the largest girl asked, leaning toward them and offering a green cardboard pint container filled with deep red berries. Carol thought of the strawberries she bought at the grocery store, their color not quite red, the ends like white bumpy skin because they were not allowed to stay ripening in the sun.

"Picked this morning," said the smaller girl. "Real fresh. And we washed 'em."

They were small, blonde and a little tattered looking, as if they spent much of their time watching out for themselves. The littlest one had several ratty spots in her hair and the remains of breakfast on the front of a t-shirt too large for her. Her older sister wore clothes a bit too small, one button left open on her shorts and a shirt that rested well above her navel.

"Well, those look just lovely," Rob said, bending down to look and then dropping onto one knee. Carol watched as he leaned his nose into the container and took a deep sniff.

"And they smell fresh." The girls both nodded at him with serious expressions, their eyes clearly content with the quality of their produce.

"We barely got out of the patch." On the table were ten, pint containers, several hours of picking and it wasn't even eight o'clock. They had to have been out before sunrise.

"You've certainly done a nice job." They beamed at him, nodding and rocking forward on their toes. The smallest one began combing her hair with her fingers, tugging gently at the snarls, but never taking her eyes off Rob. "And I'll tell you what I'm gonna do. Finish my walk with this very pretty and pregnant lady." He nodded in Carol's direction and their solemn eyes rested on her for just a moment. "Then I'll come back and buy some of these perfect berries."

"Deal," said the oldest, reaching out and grabbing Rob in a business handshake, almost Wall Street worthy. "We'll save you some. How many? They're three dollars a pint."

"Is that a good market price? Could I buy them at the P&C for less?"

"Maybe, but they wouldn't be as fresh. Those ride in trucks and get hot. Sometimes moldy." The older girl folded her arms across her chest then, prepared to wait.

"Ok, ok. I'm sold. Save me four."

Back at the house they drank some water and stood at the window watching her parents in their gardening hats move up and down rows, patting, pulling. Her mother dropped handfuls of beans into a basket while her father gathered weeds and fussed with sprinklers.

"That sure takes a lot of time," Rob said, nodding toward the garden. "I'm gonna go take a shower." He gave her shoulder a squeeze and headed out of the room. Carol stepped away too, thinking about a bowl of cereal.

"Do you want me to ride back with you after?" she asked over the top of the refrigerator door.

"Where?"

"To get the strawberries."

"Oh," he chuckled. "From those girls, the dirty ones on the hill? You didn't really think I was going to buy them?" He stopped when he saw her face.

"But you told them." Her voice rose to a shout and she slammed the refrigerator door, taking an angry step toward him. "You promised them!"

"To get us moving again," he said, as if it were the most obvious thing in the world. "What is up with you?"

She threw herself at him then, fists raised, her voice stuck in her throat. But he grabbed her by the wrists, spinning her away from him and held her while she struggled. Suddenly the only thing that mattered was to get him off of her, not touching her.

"Ok," she sobbed, sinking further toward the floor. "Just go."

He released her slowly, backing away as if she might go wild again at any moment, but stopped to whisper in her ear. "You're a fucking nut job."

She stayed with him until the end of her pregnancy,

let him place the brittle ice chips between her lips and rub her back while she struggled to breathe. His was the first hand to touch Jackson. But she never again allowed herself to feel at ease around him or in the house they shared. When she moved out, she found a small place outside her hometown, a few miles from her parents. It backed up to a creek and had a garden already settled in back. She wasn't proud of her decision, of the hour she had to travel to bring Jackson to the meeting point with his father, or of the new woman who buckled him into the car seat for the drive back to what should have been their home. Her parents didn't ever understand, although they loved having Jackson nearby; she never tried to explain, unsure if she was protecting their opinion of Rob or their opinion of her, but it ended up not mattering. She learned that some things were rotten at the center and you couldn't always tell right away. At least that was how she dealt with her shame and loneliness, consoling herself about a choice gone bad. And she remembered the strawberries.

When she pulled the car off the pavement that day and stepped out into the settling puffs of dust, they still stood by the side of the road. Their table arrayed now with only eight boxes.

"Can I have the four you were saving?"

The older girl glared at her.

"Where's he? He was supposed to come back."

They waited with accusing eyes; the younger one reached out and put her hands over the four boxes they set aside for Rob. Her nails looked frayed, like yarn and filled with dirt. Carol could feel the pulse of a headache in her left temple, a creeping line of pain that might soon have her in bed with an ice pack. In this stand-off, the choice hung before her like the ripest apple, to explain to them, maybe protect them from trusting someone like Rob again. It would certainly make her feel better, to release this story, share it with someone, shock them with his cruel lie.

"He sent me instead."

"Ok." And with that they dropped it, reached out together for the money. "Twelve dollars," they quoted in unison. She began eating on the drive home, one sweet berry after an-

36

other. The juice dripped toward her chin and she circled her tongue around the outskirts of her lips to catch it all. Smiling and tossing the ends out the open window, she fed them to her baby.

Field Burning

When Marilyn was a toddler her father let her play in the heat of spring planting without a shirt, like a boy. It felt easy, shoulders in the sun, the tiny nubs on her chest open to the world. The autumn she was eleven, an October snow surprised the farmers. Buried leaves bled orange and red and auburn in footprints, so they seemed to walk around their fields with lacerated toes. The men spent one afternoon burning off a field and a wall of brush piled along its eastern perimeter. After lunch she moved out through the tender melting snow and stood in their half circle where the flames threw heat like a blanket. She could hear the droning appetite of the fire and in its moments of swallowing silence, the river far away and rushing like a skipped heartbeat. She grew warmer and warmer as the bottle passed amongst the talk of the men and they fell into their stories and curses as if she wasn't there. She had no story to tell them, nothing to offer the sacred circle of their fire ending. So she watched the flames, felt the roar of destruction on her face and finally, swaying and elated, she threw off the turtleneck and thick wool sweater her mother made her wear. She danced and stomped on her clothes in the dirty snow and felt the heat, sizzling at her skin.

But the offering went unnoticed, for a barn cat interrupted her celebration when it shot through the inferno, yowling and alight, its tail and hind fur just turning to flames with the speed of its rush. The watching men laughed as it stumbled, wild-eyed and blinded by smoke in to their circle, its lungs full of thick, dying fear. Marilyn's father, with a flick of the pitchfork in his plump, grimy hands, sent it back into the flames, squealing and twisting where he held it on a nest of burning weeds. She stopped her bolting, mad dance with the cat's first cries and stood watching, still half naked as the smell of burning hair rose like streamers on the fire's waves and the thrashing ceased. In the second of seeing the cat still in its body, she knew it was the gray one with the blistery eye and a litter of kittens buried in the empty horse stall of the small barn. Shivering took over her body and the smell of burning meat filled the air; she tasted the sooty brine of tears and felt her voice rise in a shriek to envelop their cruelty like a noose.

They noticed then, a surprised and staring circle of men, eyes widening at the reality of her young skin.

The sharp hiss of her grandfather's voice sliced the smoke, "Look at her," then, "get her away, you ought to be ashamed."

The numbing weight of her father's field coat landed on her shoulders, and he prodded her roughly on the backside with the handle of his pitchfork, "Get to the house." They turned away and closed, her departure guaranteed; but she stayed silently for a few more minutes and watched until the white ashy skeleton of the cat crumbled into the fire's ruins.

Copper Heart

Her voice on the phone does not surprise me. It is my birthday, a time for sisters to call, to remember. But this has not always happened; details keep her away, busy, trapped. After hello she will not speak above a whisper, a steady, low drone like bees or the mumbled prayers of monks. I have to move away from my family and the TV to hear her. In the dark of my dining room, a table she has never sat around during the twelve years I have lived here, I listen as she describes her drawings of the lake where she plans to kill herself. This has been our story for years. There are sixty-eight pages in the sketch book she says, proud and possessed by this fact. In the background I can hear the turning and shifting of paper.

"I am here now," she says, her voice near sleep. And I look through the curtains to my backyard where darkness has cloaked the trees, canceled all shadows. In California, three hours away, she stares at a disc of late afternoon sun over this body of water she has selected. She does not remember it is my birthday. The tremble in her voice, a small hitch at the end of each sentence like a limp on a very old woman, makes me believe she will do as she says. When I hang up the phone, she will put down her pen, back down the access road and hit the accelerator. The last page of her sketchbook shows the car partially submerged.

"My copper heart floats out the window when I go down."

I think of the letters she has sent me over the years, the margins packed with hearts and knives, chainsaws and hypoder-mic needles. These images are the wallpaper of our days.

"I need it to stop making so much noise." In spite of the miles, the prairies and mountains that separate us, I can see her desperate eyes, darting insects against a screen. I have been
40

here before, yet the stiff fear in my throat is new. I bring words as always: some mountain hike on my last visit, the childhood nights at our lake house when we watched raccoons dig through the garbage and laughed until dawn, the German lessons she told me she was going to start at the Community College. Finally, I remind her of her grandson, living with his dad only an hour from her. The holidays are near. She stops speaking. A soft hiccup travels the dark corridor between us.

Then a pen scratching. I try to picture slender black lines dissecting the field of white as she conjures her next move.

Witched

My sister, the witch, took me in when I needed to hide from my husband, needed to heal and bandage myself back to health. After a twelve-hour trip, I walked the two miles from the bus stop to her house just before dawn, and she handed me a mug of tea at the door.

"The hiding spell is ready," Aggie said and asked no questions.

For the first few weeks, she did most of the bandaging in the form of feeding me: fresh raspberries with whole milk on cereal, frittatas from the eggs she gathered each morning, a thick vegetable soup served icy cold like gazpacho, but packed with rosemary and chopped garlic that slid down my throat like a milkshake of nutrients. For months, I lived on pretzels and diet coke, now and then throwing a frozen dinner in the microwave and then picking at it, alone in the townhouse, while Steve worked late and went out to dinner almost every night with clients. She surrounded me with flavor and texture from her garden, making me swell like I was one of her pumpkins ripening in the dirt.

Each night she tucked me into bed after sprinkling my pillowcase with an oil for dreams. A lavender softness filled my head as I breathed in the smell of campfires, fresh cilantro from the herb garden just outside, and the plush smell of trapped sunshine. Every window in the house was cleaned with newspaper and apple cider vinegar, so the morning sun came like arrows of light into all the dark corners. I woke each morning to dogs leaping down the stairs, and Aggie in the kitchen already pouring us coffee. My normal nightmares ran from a house so full of seeds and joy and wind. My bruises faded, and I stopped jumping at every banging door or raised voice.

"You have some weeding to do in the garden today,"

she told me, a few weeks after my arrival. "The tomatoes and peppers need extra hands so they're ready by the full moon." I smiled as I nodded, noticing how she spoke to me as she spoke to her teenage sons and husband. We were her labor, and I was happy to be healthy enough, by her standards, to join in.

Both hands covered in dirt, I wiped sweat from my face with a shrug of my shoulder and felt streams rivulet down my body like I was a melting glacier. After the first few minutes of pulling weeds from the black earth, I learned to place the worms back carefully without shuddering too much and eased the disturbed dirt back over the roots, patting it down as I worked. The rows looked endless as I switched from tomatoes to peppers and realized my nephews already finished their assigned spaces. They ran past in swimsuits, headed for the lake on the edge of Aggie's property as I worked the final row, jalapeno plants with blossoms already smelling of heat.

"Pretty passable," Aggie said, waiting where the dirt met green, a sweating glass of amber tea in her hand. "Help me pick arugula and kale for our salad and you're done for the day."

Her busy, summer-work household was exactly what I needed as cobblers and pickles came to life in her kitchen, and I began to think about how to move ahead. Produce of some kind sat on the counter every day, changing colors as the weeks went by. We chopped and froze green beans, then cut corn from the cob and canned the peaches we gathered in her orchard. We ate it all too, but the miracle of those jars and packages, how sure she was of a family to feed through the winter, how safe in the promise of having those she loved around her when the cold season took hold, were the facts that most amazed me. This daily love affair with the ground on which she walked, her morning meditations and evening Wiccan prayers, spoke to me of a hope I knew had never been in my life.

By early October, the nights were too cool to sleep with the windows open, and I missed the sun's heat on my neck when I worked my morning garden hours. We dug the root vegetables to store in stainless steel washtubs: potatoes, carrots, and parsnips, just the two of us bringing in the harvest with the boys back at school.

"They keep best in the dirt. And I love digging them out during a blizzard, like my garden keeps going." She finished speaking, then shifted onto her heels and stretched her back. I dumped two perfect potatoes into the washtub on my right, their skins cool from the ground and covered in wet dirt. Could these two wind up in a stew I would eat? A breeze carried the smell of basil to my nose as Aggie stood and pinched some from the herbs that lined the rows and kept mosquitoes and asparagus beetles away, according to this sister of mine who seemed to understand the connections between every living thing. It felt like an answer; I was staying here, my life now close to these rows.

"For as long as you like," Aggie said. She raised her hands above her head, then dropped into a sun salutation, one of her many spontaneous stretch and give thanks moves I watched all summer.

My husband, Steve, pulled into the driveway that afternoon while I was checking the pumpkin patch on the side of the barn closest to the house. At first, I thought he hadn't seen me, might not be certain he found me. So, I tucked myself behind the old apple tree as he climbed from his car, but the sun glinted off the gun in his hand as he slammed the door. Immediately I stepped into view to steer him from the house.

"Thought you were safe here playing farmer?" His grin was as sneering as I remembered. Aggie told me the spell for hiding would not last forever, would weaken as I gained strength and my energy made its way back into the streams of life around me. That he stayed away this long was a blessing I accepted too easily. I could not take my eyes off the gun as he moved toward me across the yard. While I stared, he got closer and then seemed to freeze in place, not even ten feet from where I stood beneath the apple tree. His foot slowly lowered to the ground, but his body grew still, almost slack. Aggie's voice filled my ears then, a babbling run of syllables I couldn't understand until she screamed from the porch. "Run Tess."

I couldn't move. He looked dreadful, unshaven and thin, his hair graying along the temples in a way that made him look old, rather than distinguished. His shirt was buttoned incorrectly, one side hanging down almost to his knees, and that scared me most of all; the Steve I knew would never leave the house, much less drive across three states, dressed in such a disheveled way.

Instead of running, I turned to face Aggie on the porch and saw her arms raised, a sort of electric energy coming off her in blue, shuddering waves that surrounded Steve where he stood. But even as I watched, I could see it loosening, the color fading and the aura growing thin, like a soap bubble before popping. Steve straightened, his move a flash in the corner of my eye as he too turned toward Aggie.

"You fucking bitch," he yelled, his voice thick and unclear, like he'd just had Novocain at the dentist. He raised his arm, the gun now pointing at Aggie. It all happened in slow motion as the last of her energy waves faded. I jumped at him, hit him from behind, grabbing around the waist and pulling down as I fell. Caught by surprise, he collapsed, and I heard the gun fire as my chin hit the grass and rattled my teeth. He twisted on top of me almost immediately, his weight as familiar as my own pulse in my ears. This was always how it was going to end. And then I was screaming as he pulled my hair and my neck popped backward. He straddled me, keeping the pressure on my neck. I could see the porch where Aggie should have been but wasn't. Then I felt cold pressed against my temple and Steve's heavy breathing, as he settled himself across my back and pulled a little tighter on my ponytail. I recognized this moment of him just about to fire, almost like I saw it in a dream. He growled at me from behind, but I couldn't make out the words.

Then his weight disappeared, lifted, and I was free. He dropped his grip on my hair. As I rolled over to see where he had gone, the gun thunked down beside my head. Above me Steve's legs kicked and scrambled, his body suspended off the ground; the limbs of the apple tree twined around him. The tree lifted him while he screeched and tried to struggle loose. Between leaves and the black strength of branches, his face looked bleached, his eyes deep buckets of fear as they met mine. For only a moment, he dangled at the full height of the tree. Where the massive trunk stood, I heard a cracking and creaking. In seconds a hollowed section in the trunk appeared. The branches holding my still screaming husband shifted again, and I watched as the tree shoved him toward its base, took him in. As Steve vanished, the hole filled itself and was sealed off, the bark somehow knitting itself back together.

I ran to the spot, touched the place where he had just been. Somewhere far away, deep behind the space that I knew had been open a moment before, an echo of Steve's voice. Above my head, the branches returned to normal, leaves shaking in the breeze, a picture of October innocence that made me doubt all I saw. Breathing too fast and stumbling away from the tree, I started toward Aggie on the porch.

She was on her back, a hand up to her shoulder, a pool of red beside her as she stared at the porch roof and mumbled the syllables I heard in her mouth all summer. Her other hand did not return my grip, but her eyes shifted to mine.

"There's a new jar of moss in the medicine cabinet." It took me a moment to realize she had switched to English. "Go."

Back on the porch with the jar, I could only stare at the pool of blood growing larger until she opened her eyes again. The deep dirt smell filled my nose as I dumped the jar's contents. The moss was green and velvet smooth, each piece about the size of a slice of bread, but thicker. I placed one on her shoulder; she groaned when it contacted the wound, but instantly it seemed to wrap itself around her, molding to her shape while a sucking noise began. On the boards of the porch, the blood, just moments before seeping out, reversed and crept back toward Aggie's shoulder. It was like a movie played in reverse, and with this motion came the strange noise, not human, but nearly; I could not stop feeling like the moss was somehow sucking her back to health, back in time, back to a place before the gunshot. Of course, it wasn't possible, but possible had become a wider set of options in the last few minutes, and I couldn't deny the color slowly easing back into her face. The flush of hours in the sun and the deep lines edging out from her years of laughter, filled back in with their normal tanned color. It couldn't be happening, but then again, my husband could not possibly have been sucked into the body of a tree just moments before he killed me. None of it could be true. When Aggie sat up, the piece of moss dropped into her hand with a plopping sound, and she stood, without any effort or struggle, carrying it immediately to the side of the porch to twist it like a wet rag.

"Much better." She turned with a face far too normal. "I need to get some potatoes baking for dinner."

"Are we not going to talk about that?" I swept my hand across the lawn, ending with the tree.

"It will be easier not to." She crossed her arms and leaned back against the porch railing, as if the decision rested with me. Before I could answer, a rumbling noise began on the side of the house. We both reached the top of the porch steps at the same time and moved together toward the noise. At the corner where her driveway began, the rumble grew louder. On the graveled surface, a huge sink hole opened around Steve's car. As quickly as the tree patched him into its trunk, the driveway collapsed around the Lexus; the gravel and dirt beneath his tires suddenly vanished, only to reappear exactly like a zipper would pull two sides of a suitcase together.

"Problem solved," Aggie said.

We ate turkey chili on baked potatoes that night, my appetite difficult to find, but Aggie's eyes reassured me. Calm and certain, she nodded when I picked up my fork, smiled at me between the flickering light of candles set in the middle of the table. We were five, gathered in late October twilight, eating together as a family.

Brother

When Anna was five, she pretended to watch Belle in her yellow gown bring the forgotten castle to life. The movie, a magic dilemma of unruly furniture and songs, couldn't hold her attention. Really she waited for her parents and the new baby brother she felt kick against her hand when she pressed it gently to her mother's skin, tight and stretched like a face against glass. It seemed like days at Aunt Mary's waiting for news from the hospital; finally her dad came and said this brother would not stay with them, *could* not stay because he was sick, like her cat had been sick and had gone to heaven.

"I can't even tell you how sick," he said, his forehead resting against hers until she could feel each ridge of the skin above his eyes. When he sighed, everything ended in a shudder and she smelled a hot, grown-up smell, like the diner where he sometimes took her for breakfast.

"Then Mommy will." She reached for his hand, his fingers thick and rough from the nails he pounded all day, the walls he told her about connecting together, until a house stood where it hadn't stood before. "It's ok not to know, Daddy. Aunt Mary says things take time."

So she waited for the brother who could not stay, and she tried to watch Belle's dress twirl in a fog around her happiness. In the kitchen Aunt Mary and the other adults talked over cigarettes, their voices prowling like cats. Her daddy kissed the top of her head and stood up, just as the Beast in his blue suit became a prince. From the corner of her eye, Anna saw her mother sneak through the room, a bundle clutched against her chest, a secret to hide.

"How did you get here?" Anna shouted, leaping to her feet. She felt her father's fingers choke her arm and she dropped to her knees, slipped through his grasp. She dove at her mother,

48

needing to hug her, to touch her, not just the thought of her. But her mother's palm met her chest, shoved her away.

"Keep her back." Her mother screamed and for just a moment, the blanket slipped. Anna saw the shadow of a face, a scrambled, mixed around face like the pieces of a puzzle not put together. She must have blinked she would tell herself even years later when, lying in her bed as a teenager, the image would press itself deep in her mind. This moment of a face was all she ever had to call brother, to know a sibling of any kind, and she learned quickly how to keep the secret locked away in its own tower. And then her father caught her in his arms, his palms tough and clumsy through the fabric of her nightgown. They landed together on the couch in a tight bear hug that she struggled to break.

"It's ok, it's ok," he whispered and held her. Opening her eyes there was only the empty room and the blank screen where Belle lived happily ever after.

Beneath the Skin

She peeled an orange and found an avocado, the sort of week it had been. The feel of buttery green on her tongue failed to be what she needed as she ate it. Between trips to the cleaners, the library, the morgue, she held her hands steady on the wheel— the grip of an adult, certain and not trembling, her gaze definitely not looking left at the swish of angels, their wings like a coat of rain across the grass.

In the driveway, her phone growled its string of small curses, and she took deep breaths before going in to fill the muffin tins with batter, organic blueberries, her tears. For years there had been somewhere else to drive, someone else to taxi, someplace else to be, until there wasn't. Now the vacuum carved its licorice lines along the carpet, and she refused to move the cushions or look beneath the couch, afraid of what might have worked its way there to lie forever, to speak a silent lie—family. Some small barrette or the game socks from soccer season that went missing weeks before, these were risks she could not take. By afternoon she was dustbowl empty. She thought up other errands to run. In the garage, no end it seemed to jump ropes and scooters, a whale sprinkler she could picture as it spun its lazy circle on the lawn.

She thought she might siphon such wreckage forever, or at least until daylight passed and she could pretend to sleep. It felt necessary to find objects that took up space, fill in the space where air refused to stay when she shook out leaf bags and tried to line them up.

"That's a lot of trash," her husband said meaning the eleven bags she deposited on the curb. She did not answer. A square aluminum pan came out of the oven; peeling back the foil, she uncovered macaroni and cheese. It might have been anything they gathered on the shiny tines of their forks and moved toward their mouths. They ate because he was home from work, and she put utensils down on placemats. In bed when clocks reported it was time, she lay still as lists pushed their way up like new mountains, a continent, she hoped, of details. She could feel the slow breaths beside her, a game of sleep they might play all night. Hours later, she moved toward him with moonlight and darkness in slats across the bed. On his skull, skin met hair in a smoothed edge, like the orange of her morning. Somewhere along this expanse, it might be possible to break through and slide her fingers beneath the careful surface. When he remained still despite her touch, she dug her nails in and peeled away the rind of silence and blame that covered his face. He was hollow where the heat of him should have been. Time and their grief ripened only to this husk she could sweep away without effort.

Marigold Hill

The hill, school bus yellow with marigolds in bloom, was part of the Marset farm. On Hank's morning drive, he passed it, watched it come to life that spring like the sidewalk borders and front garden of Ellen's house. She lived three blocks from the high school but rode in his truck when he pulled to the curb, her two friends flanking her so all of them could take a drive around town before pulling into school to sit through another day. There were times when he wanted to be more alone with her, to venture toward his thoughts and uncomfortable dreams, but he was not good with words or asking questions, so the girls' chatter each morning made the ride easy in a way it would not have been. Plus, four across the front seat pushed her tight against him; their legs and hips, ribs and shoulders aligned and connected.

"My parents won't be home 'til 9 Thursday night. We could go somewhere," she said, sliding out of the truck one morning. The ends of her hair fell like a soft veil. Her words, just above a whisper, sounded like the quiet nickering of horses. There was nothing to do but nod.

At school on Thursday, each class droned on, no distinction in his mind between the numbers he punched into his calculator and the amendments he identified on his quiz. After chores, a shower and some gel on the cowlick he could never control, he drove to pick her up. The road between his parent's farm and town felt fifty miles long as early summer twilight edged toward the sunset that would soon wash the sky. The hill would be beautiful. In the fall she would go away to college, two states away in a small city he never visited. He knew he should take her to a hotel, but there was only the Microtel out near the interstate forty minutes away or the bed and breakfast run by their English teacher's wife. She sighed at their options the night before, accepting the hill and leaning in to kiss him, then flutter her hand across his chest.

* * *

Her younger brother shot baskets in the driveway. They nodded as he climbed the front steps. Before he could knock, she stepped onto the porch in a dress he had never seen. As they drove out of town, she held his hand and hummed with the radio.

When he parked on the shoulder, they heard the crunch of gravel through the open window and the quiet pings of the engine. From the bed of the truck he grabbed a scratchy wool blanket and his old scout canteen, now filled with his mother's chardonnay.

"Those shoes might be a problem," he said, opening her door. She climbed out, one foot in the high weeds where grasshoppers swayed on the heads of Queen Anne's lace. The high-heeled sandals she wore looked unstable.

"Should I take them off?"

"Too much to step on. We'll go slow." Putting his keys in his pocket, he headed into the tall grass.

"What if someone sees?" He stopped to wait for her, held out his empty hand as she took a wobbly step.

"Nobody out here."

They reached a fence at the far edge of the cow pasture. He climbed under then parted the rusty barbed wire, threw the blanket on the grass and turned to help her. Moving from foot to foot, she twitched her fingers through the ends of her hair, didn't reach for him.

"Coming?" He didn't mean to sound impatient. She took a step and bent down. Unused to such maneuvers, she attempted to rise before clearing the fence. The high hump of her spine scratched along one barbed point. Shrieking, she fell forward and knocked them both in a pile to the ground. As they rolled and struggled, she swung at him. He caught her arm, subduing her in a grip that drove an ax through wood and hoisted hay bales. Separately they coughed out dust.

Her back to him, she trembled and took in heavy

53

breaths. He could see the rip in her sundress, a line of blood soaking into the fabric from a short, jagged scratch.

"Wanna go back?" Sincerity, for he wouldn't feel right, might really love her. But she shook her head no. She spent the first weekends of summer weather watching the other girls notice him when they hung out at the beach on Saturdays, how strong his legs were, his chest almost pressed against her as they lay talking on their towels. She knew others wanted him, was pretty sure she loved him. It was time.

At the hill, he held her hand again, threaded them up the trail of gold, flower upon flower, thick as a carpet. Settling them on the blanket, he offered her wine from the round mouth of the canteen and leaned in to kiss the vibrating silk of her neck while she drank. She sputtered, pushed the canteen away and reached for him. They were never this alone before. His hand moved just beneath her dress and reached her thigh; he lowered her and settled above, his movements more certain than he felt. As her back made full contact with the blanket, she gasped, the pain from her scrape unexpected. In the pause he kissed her again, trying to be gentle.

"Have you got…? He searched his pocket, wondering how he could have forgotten, his mind racing with surprise. They lacked grace, but fumbled through, a clumsy sweetness as they dismantled clothes, adjusted, wondered how it all worked without ever speaking. It surprised her finally with a sharp bite of pain in the fading light. For him the surprise was how familiar it seemed. They both looked for what might have changed, he at the phosphorescence of marigolds in the day's dying light, she at the blood orange sky stretched overhead toward forever.

Thirty Love

I remember how we touched eventually, all our skin, only a few clothes to remove since it was summer, too hot for tennis or spoken love. But we met on the court because you left a note on my windshield; *Courts at 4*. And beside your name a quick sketch of a racquet, a speech bubble—*meet me*. I wanted to be a bit late, minutes for you to wonder if I would show, but it hadn't worked. At 4:15 you parked your car, and I had to pretend I just arrived. We knocked at the ball despite the heat. You practiced your big serve to measure out your strength and left a deep bruise on my thigh. I lost on purpose, ignored the pain, smiled to stay with you, and hoped there was time planned for afterwards. We took your car to a second-floor apartment just off campus, the back of an old college town Victorian. You weren't living there, just squatting in a friend's rental—a temporary thing, like the summer's warm, guzzled beer.

You placed me on the porch floor scratchy with sand. Magazines stacked and leaning by an old couch, I thought of all the advice columns and articles almost at my fingertips. Still dressed, we explored around our clothes. Your lips just brushed the space between my neck and shoulders, hot breath on hot skin, until I lifted my t-shirt overhead. A lawn mower stumbled alive, and a June bug hit the door's screen again, again, again. I wanted to be bored by it all but wasn't. Breezes shifted the bamboo blinds. Your body moved above me, light and dark, empty, full, forward and back, a deep rush I knew even then was just the sun's clever trick of time.

List of Contacts

Any phone call after midnight is a cause for nerves, but tonight I am alone, my husband on a fishing trip with our son. I answer the house phone with toothpaste on the corners of my mouth, snatching it from its stand on the bedside table. In the near second of silence while the line engages, I imagine catastrophe as it explodes like the red and white of fireworks inside my head.

"Hello?" All I want is to hear Matt's voice.

"Yes, hello. Sorry to call so late. I'm looking for Matthew Harder," says the voice, an older man it seems.

"He isn't here, can I take a message?" Do I really mean this at ten minutes after midnight? And how does he know Matt?

"But he does live there?" His voice drops then, so I can only hear a mumble, then a loud blast of sound. I think he has just blown his nose. "Again, I'm sorry. I'm looking for Matthew Harder."

"It's late. Do you want to leave him a message?"

There is crying now on the other end of the line, wet sobs and rattling breath. I sit down on my bed to listen. The mattress cradles me as I wait.

"Do you know Brian Galston? Or know how Matthew Harder knows him?" I am getting annoyed now.

"Do you want to leave a message or not?"

"He's my son. My only son," says this voice on a phone in an unknown location. Some thread of his pain reaches me, and I think of Parker, picture him curled in a sleeping bag beside a stream in the shadow of Cat Mountain. Like this voice on the phone, I also have a son, an only son, whose arm at this moment could be thrown into the cold of the tent with some chocolate from his 'smore still on his lips.

"I'm sorry. I haven't ever heard his name before." The phone has the hush of a room emptied by decades and covered in dust. He might have hung up, until his voice struggles back, captured like a creature in the woods and then free on the end of the line, careening around in its agony.

"He's dead," he says before repeating the animal noises. "I'm in his apartment and what am I supposed to do?" I have no answer. Words form in my head: *Because I could not stop for death*. I regret my Emily Dickinson semester and English major background as I look at the framed photos of my family on the bedside table. Hang up the phone and dismiss him I tell myself but feel heartless. Then just as quickly, I forgive the hard callous of my thoughts because I am afraid of what he faces, too overcome to let any molecule of his grief touch me. The moment has me trapped, a collision in slow motion that I cannot force out of my view.

"I'm going through his address book, his contacts," he says when I can't quite cut the connection. "So, I started at A and haven't found anyone who can tell me what happened. Most don't even answer their phones. When did people stop answering their phones? It's the middle of the night. Who could ignore the phone ringing in the middle of the night?"

He makes a good point; the sound echoes in all of my nightmares, never a good reason to get a call like this.

"I'm sorry. I don't know how to help you."

"Nobody does. I'll reach Z in this damn book without any help. He was twenty-six years old."

There is no other thing to say, no claim to make or soothing word-like balm to offer him.

"The police took him, took his body and left me this empty space, some life he didn't want in a city he didn't know. Who let this happen?"

Again, I say, "I'm sorry." In the silence on the line that stretches like taut elastic, ready to snap, I find myself clutching the quilt with my free hand, fingers locked around fabric as if it could matter, could redeem all I have not even lost. But I have lost, here and now in this exchange I cannot end, I have seen all the days I will wait for a moment like this to arrive. This voice becomes a vision of my future, and I want to throw the phone down because it scalds my hand with this nightmare I am allowing myself to try on.

"I taught him to shoot when he was ten. Took him to the woods. The spike horns of his first deer are on the wall in my basement. I didn't even know he had a gun. I used to know everything about him, and now all I can find are memories of a stranger. What can I tell his mother?"

It does not seem to matter if I speak. And I am afraid if I open my mouth I will scream or accuse him of heaping all this pain onto me. If only Matt were here. Answering this man should be his responsibility, not mine.

"I've taken too much of your time." His voice changes, suggests that he has shaken himself out; the image of his gray hair and flannel shirt that has been developing as I have listened to him suddenly straightens, his shoulders lift and resettle. He will move around the planet differently from now on.

"It's ok," I lie. I will get off this phone and drive an hour through the dark to the parking lot where Matt will have left our van. I will wait there until daylight and then move along the trail to Cat Mountain until I find their tent.

"Thank you for answering."

"If you leave me a number I can ask Matt about your son."

"No. I've troubled you enough."

The line, suddenly dead, shocks me. "Hello? Hello?" I cannot believe he simply hung up; I shake the phone and stare at it, press the id button to examine his number. I could call him back on my cell, could try to find out where he is. Something needs to be done for this man I now envision as he prowls around his dead son's apartment, growing desperate for information he can probably never find. The area code is not familiar to me as I type it into my cell and add it to my contact list, "father of the dead man who knows Matt." I cannot even recall his son's name from our conversation. But I am glad to have this number. It is quite possible I will call on the drive to Cat Mountain; he will certainly answer.

Retail

Customers saunter by as clouds before the sun; I wish for a slingshot to shoot out their eyes. Corduroy ribs the skin on my arms, and packaged angora smells like a science project of formaldehyde and empty veins. Incessant dance music like my head in a hive and the bass drum beat of credit cards sliding into action.

I hide the garlic from lunch with a breath saver, for that open mouth smile. Dust balls are the shuffle of feet on a blind woman's grave. But we must fold and clean and straighten. Some days all I do is vacuum the detritus of unclothed customers, the sloughing of skin as they pull on their jeans. I want to call in sick today, really feel sick today from air-filtered cologne and the slick nausea of near naked models on posters the size of small gods. Did George Washington ever wear jeans? The new season of democracy lives in pastels.

At the fitting room door, she asks, "Do you know when these will be on sale?

Moments later, "Do they make me look hippy? Because I just lost ten pounds and plan on ten more."

"Not at all," I lie while the empty dressing room of morals slams its door for good.

Customer one raises her arms and floats to the ceiling, a new form of shoplifting. My manager pulls on her heels, wondering if she has the store credit card and what its limit might be.

"Catch her," we scream, our arms waving empty hangers and sensors we have removed all morning. I think of the new stock waiting in its plastic, the rest of "back to school" even though it is barely July. She would descend for a look at fall's hot sweater. But I envy her attitude, want my own soggy feet off the floor. Then I could grow fat with the answers to argyle questions. Or maybe quit this job and live here forever. It is time for my break. Now I am the cloud in the competition's window, hearing a parade of stone-washed denim call my name.

Table for Two

"Table for two," the phrase had not stopped echoing in Sarah's head since she read it on the receipt while cleaning off the counter and drinking her morning coffee. It was in a pile with other papers and the change Kyle took it out of his pocket in a hurry to get to the airport. It was a rush like every morning in their weekday lives, frantic and hands thrown in the air, misplaced, out of place, never ready when the clock said it was time to go. He kissed her only an hour ago with the garment bag draped across his shoulder and his computer case on wheels between them. Lips just brushed, no arms or body pressed together, perfunctory at best, reluctant now in her mind as she looked again at the receipt.

On Saturday he called the evening a work dinner, networking, old friends he hadn't seen in several years from the project he worked on. Names rattled off: Kim, Anthony, Andrew, Natalie.

"Is it a couple thing?" she asked, knowing she hadn't showered after the gym and was planning to sink into the couch with a glass of wine and several episodes of Grey's Anatomy. Had he seemed worried then, looking too quickly to convince her? Nothing made her think so.

"No, just the group. Some of them don't even have a half, you know? Social bullshitting. A few hours." And he had gone up to take his own shower, then played a quick round of Battleship with Franny who couldn't get enough of the game since Christmas and left, in jeans, a striped shirt and his casual blue blazer. She hadn't started pacing the floor until midnight. Dinner in D.C. should take at most three hours, plus thirty minutes in and out. He left at 6:40; she was sure of this because she always paid attention to such things, had been paying attention most of her life to the departures of her loved ones. It wasn't her fault, the therapist assured her and mostly, Kyle was kind about it.

She shared the event that spawned her lifetime of concern on their sixth date, two after they slept together. It was a measure of trust for her in those days, the most important sort of trust, to let someone know how her mother died. It shocked people at first, getting hit by a tire that flew off a car at the Onondaga Speedway, freak accident, bad luck. But the most shocking of all was the coma she lived in for fourteen years. Sarah was five when it happened, could still remember the halter top her mother was wearing—blue denim with sequins that flashed in the sun when she opened the front door, swinging her purse over her shoulder and looking back to blow Sarah a kiss. Her father was only a step behind, and he patted his wife on the butt, right in front of Sarah, as he left. She could hear her mother's giggle, the very last sound she would ever hear her make on her own. The next time Sarah saw her, she was lying in a hospital bed with tubes and wires connected, all of her beautiful blonde hair gone. Her scalp was red and rough, scraped to bleeding. From the eyes up, she looked like a skinned knee in need of a bandage.

All of this she told Kyle while he ran his fingers gently up and down her spine, working the story from her with the magic of his touch. She took it as a sign that she could get through the entire experience without crying for the first time. And once they were married, he made a point to call her before he left work, would not stay out of touch for long periods of time, reached out the minute his plane was on the ground when he flew because he knew how she watched the news for Special Reports and checked Yahoo every few minutes because a plane crash would be listed there almost instantly. Part of her believed she would know when the worst happened, when what she always expected to happen, someone in her family being ripped from her, became a reality. It would happen when she wasn't thinking about it, when she let down her guard. And so, she thought about it always. Ran the list of those she loved through her mind each night in a litany of prayer and she paced, checked windows, the TV, the computer and moved around trying to focus on other things, while some section of her brain carried on with its worrying.

Nut brown Ale
Sam Adams Seasonal
Pinot Noir
Grande Nachos
Pinot Noir
Sam Adams Seasonal

Three beers and two glasses of wine, plus nachos-- an evening of hours measured out by drinks, clear as could be on the receipt. And up near the date and the server's name, Kate, it said "party of 2." When she first found it and began reading, putting a story together, it felt like some strange mistake. The date wrong in her mind maybe? He traveled to Chicago the week before, no doubt had dinner out. But February 17 was Saturday night, two days ago. And standing in front of the calendar she kept hung on hooks in the coat closet because she could never remember to put things in her Google calendar on her phone, her knees went weak. In a hot rush that should have been impossible, her bowels released, and she had to run for the bathroom.

This was not the sort of disaster her mind prepared for, but she spun its many implications around as she drove Franny to school and then moved herself between the dry cleaners, grocery store, gym and Jiffy Lube for the oil change she had been putting off. The receipt rode along in the pocket of her jeans, and she stared at it while she waited in line and glanced between it and the television on the wall in the waiting area that smelled like grease and hand cleaner. Each time she read it, the same bottomless feeling washed over her, and her knees would go soft at the center. By lunchtime she could picture herself leaving Kyle, packing Franny and some clothes into the van and heading for her sister's where she could stay until she was ready to move forward. Franny could join another gymnastics studio; Kyle would figure out what to do with their house. She dismantled her life as a foregone conclusion, with a clean and efficient mind. And then she cried and put it all back together for the benefit of Franny, for the utter impossibility of such a failure in her life.

Back at home, with two hours until it was time to go

after Franny, the pacing started. She would have to confront him, and it would have to be once he arrived in Denver. His flight, scheduled to arrive by 2 p.m. east coast time, had almost stayed off her mind, angry and betrayed as she was. "Just landed," said the text at 2:17. He might not answer if she called, and she stood in the middle of the family room, the TV on mute and her breath a desperate flailing animal in a cage, as she tried to decide what to do. He won every fight they ever had. And she complained to her sister about that once.

"You fight too fair," Carrie said. "You always have."

"Fair how?"

"Careful. You never let yourself get really angry, say something horrid."

"And you do?" But even as she asked she could remember bathroom arguments where Carrie would storm in and throw open the shower curtain, proclaim her right to the bathroom immediately and turn the water to cold, screaming insults and stating the obvious reasons it was her time to be in there alone.

"I don't want to say anything I need to take back. You know? What if I yell something and storm off like you do, then the person gets in a car accident or gets hit by a bus?" And Carrie laughed, called her crazy, "waiting for the other shoe always." Over the years it was how her family addressed Sarah's worrying. It was also why Kyle won every fight they ever had. It never felt worth really trying to win, plus she was afraid she might just snap and shout things that would tumble their lives to pieces like Jenga blocks on the kitchen table. He might leave, as he threatened to do on a few occasions when she tried to point out his lack of effort around the house or the fact that he never put his dishes in the dishwasher.

It would begin ok, a request she made for him to start the laundry while she was gone or maybe Kyle asking what was wrong after she sighed in the kitchen. But the escalation happened in a flash: all the work he did to keep their lives going, the hours he spent on the highway each week, the exhaustion he felt, and she would find herself pleading with him to forget she brought it up. It was important to end such discussions by reuniting, approaching him for a hug or reassurance that they were ok, but sometimes he would storm away from her, not let her touch him. A few weeks before she followed him out to the garage in January cold as he jumped in his car and backed out of the driveway. Surrounded by shovels and empty flowerpots, she yelled for him to stop, talk to her, sort it out, but the back tires threw some slush in the air, and he was gone. For the first few minutes she was angry, then immediately worried. Would he come back? Where would he go? What if something happened? She sent a text, what's happening? Then called and got voice mail. The sound of her need embarrassed her, the depth of her begging. Franny came in wanting a snack while she pleaded into the answering machine.

"What's wrong?" Franny said. Running her fingers through her daughter's hair, Sarah forced herself to take a breath, to feel the solid nine-year old body leaning into her.

Now she stood with the phone in her hand, staring at his text, desperate to know what happened, even as another part of her mind turned away and begged her to leave it alone. But she couldn't pretend it was nothing, wouldn't be that blind or fooled. The night he stormed away he also come home after two, and she forced herself to stay in bed, to lie still as he changed his clothes and took a pillow with him to the couch. She could put a string of these nights together if she let herself think back. Instead she began a text.

Troubled by a receipt I found on the counter. She pushed send, before she thought too much about it.

What receipt?

Last Saturday, your group thing for work.

??

Party of 2 at Wild Steer Brewery.

What makes you say 2?

The receipt says it. 3 beers, two glasses of wine, nachos and a party of 2.

So?

Not really your description of the night.

I don't remember what I said.

Work thing, lots of people, you named them. Said you'd only be a few hours.

The tightness in her chest was there as it always was, but she could peck out these answers without getting confused, or crying, without watching him throw his hands around or raise his voice. She could get to what she really meant to say.

What's your point?

What you told me and what you did don't match.

According to the receipt? That's your evidence?

Are you saying the receipt is wrong? The server didn't record all the people there? Missed some people?

Ten minutes later he had still not responded. Shaking and near tears, she carried the phone upstairs and made herself stow it between the mattress and box spring. She put the leash on the dog and walked around the neighborhood until it was time to get Franny. The phone stayed hidden through the rest of the afternoon because she stopped herself three times at the bottom of the stairs, each time forcing herself to take deep breaths and think about why she needed to stay away. It was an addict's conversation, a desperate stand-off with her obsession.

He called the home phone while she stared at a salad and Franny ate through her macaroni and cheese, barely chewing between stories of the baby ducks they were incubating and the kick ball game she had been included in because she could catch the ball better than her friend Ashley.

"Daddy wants you," Franny said. She held the phone out to Sarah after telling Kyle the kickball story.

"Yes?"

"Checking in. Sounds like a busy day for the girl." Sarah could not believe how normal he sounded, how could he not have images in his mind of court, boxed items, fights over who got the patio furniture? It had been so inevitable to her all afternoon, and now he sounded like Kyle, her husband, a normal night with him away on business. She couldn't make sense of it, wanted to let things slide into normalcy, but wasn't quite able to put away the list of drinks she had read.

"I have to go. Franny has a lot of math."

"It can't wait a minute? Why the rush?" He paused and she let the silence sit. "What's going on?"

She hesitated just a moment, wanted to pull back and

make everything smooth, like the comforter on their bed each day, straight and neat, the pillows fluffed, a promise they would return there at the end of the day. The finished bed was a moment of prayer for her each time she made it.

"I can't talk to you right now."

"What does that mean?" She could hear the shift away from friendly chatter; a picture of him moving into a boxing stance came to mind, his fists settling in front of his face at the black belt tournament where she cheered for him several years ago.

"I have to go." She pushed the end button and then stared at the instrument in her hand, the connection she had just broken. The regret settled in immediately, and she ran for the bathroom, the phone clattering onto the table.

He didn't call for the next two days. She held the phone in hand, almost calling every few minutes, then hours, as she grew accustomed to the silence.

* * *

Six months after the accident, the doctors took her mother off life support. She breathed on her own. For fourteen years she ate through a feeding tube, never moving or opening her eyes. There was no brain activity the medical people all agreed, so Sarah, her father and sister made a trip to the hospital each Sunday afternoon to sit with her in the room of measured exhales, tucked-in sheets and the smell of rubbing alcohol. It seemed to Sarah that a nurse was swabbing one part or another of her mother with a cotton ball every few minutes on those afternoons. As the years passed, friends and family members pointed out that it was time to move on, to let her go, but Sarah anchored herself in those gatherings, the hospital pudding she ate when she was small with its dollop of whipped cream or the hours she spent reading her English papers into the room with the rhythm of monitors in the background. Every few months, Sarah and Carrie changed the pictures that hung on a cork board above their mother's bed. They grew up on that board, shifting from sand castles and sitting on Santa's lap to Proms and packing for college. Carrie began to skip some Sundays because she was with a boyfriend and then away at school, and once Sarah got her license, sometimes her father would send her alone.

* * *

On the day after Kyle was due back in town, Franny had a gymnastics meet in Philadelphia with team warm up scheduled for 7 a.m. on Saturday morning. Early in the season Sarah booked a hotel room for Friday, not knowing Kyle would be traveling and scheduled to fly in.

Franny and I are leaving right after school for the meet. We'll be back Saturday afternoon. She hit send after reading it over three times, wondering what he might respond, where he would be when he read it. She composed texts to him four times in the days of their silence, but only sent this one. He had not called at all. In their twelve years of marriage they never went this long without speaking. And Kyle never missed one of Franny's meets. They agreed before he left that she would cancel the hotel and they'd leave by 3 a.m., drive up 95 together while Franny slept in the back.

If he didn't answer, she was wondering who she might get in touch with to be sure he was ok. Did she know the hotel he was staying at? Flight numbers, airlines, always, but why didn't she ask about the hotel? The possibilities she never worried about chased around in her thoughts like wild dogs. But something in her also felt resolve; she would not make this ok as she normally did, no matter what came next.

* * *

When she picked Franny up on Friday afternoon the car was already packed. She had snacks and several DVDs ready as they set off on the highway.

"We aren't even going home first?"

"We'll get a jump on traffic."

"What about Daddy? Is he meeting us there?"

"Not this time honey, just the girls. It'll be fun." She could taste the lie in her mouth, like dry crackers, a voice she didn't believe, and suspected Franny would doubt as well.

"Can we still eat Italian with the other girls after the meet?"

"Sure."

They were near the exit for the airport now; Kyle's

flight, if it landed on time, would settle onto the tarmac in about five hours. By then she would be in a hotel room outside Philly, probably braiding Franny's hair or maybe finishing a glass of wine at the bar with the other gymnastics moms while the girls watched Disney channel in one of the rooms. Nothing was set up to be different, except Kyle would not be there.

* * *

Her father remarried less than a month after the funeral, a woman he began dating the summer before Sarah went to college. Carrie was happy for him, went to visit and brought her kids. They all went on a trip to Disneyworld when Sarah's nephews were five and seven. Sarah and her family were invited, her father offering to pay, to let them do some of the family things they had never done.

"He missed the chance for those trips," Carrie said. "We all missed them. Can't you let it go? He wasn't cheating on her. You can't cheat on a vegetable." They were sitting at Carrie's kitchen table, the kids outside in the backyard in their bathing suits, screaming as they slid the length of the slip and slide. Sarah sat near a window and held her breath each time Franny took off running. The water spray caught sunlight and sparkled as her daughter's body sped the length of yellow plastic and she squealed. Hitting the grass, she continued to slide a few feet and then jumped up to go again.

Sarah didn't answer. After watching Franny land in the soaked grass two more times, she wrapped her in a towel and took her home. It wasn't that she was angry with her father or sister. She knew they were reasonable, supported by everyone that those years had not been well spent, that they should have taken the final steps long before they did. Sarah's sophomore year in college, Carrie newly married and pregnant, they sat her down after the Christmas presents were opened and the house was sleepy with cooking smells, to tell her the decision was made to remove the feeding tube. Dorian, her father's "friend," was in the kitchen, as she had been since Sarah arrived, possessive and directing everyone as she pulled quiche and apple pie from the oven, leaned in to kiss her father when he walked by on his way to the dining room. "Be nice," Carrie scolded each time

69

they caught each other's gaze. It was funny to Sarah that they all called her the meek one, the frightened one, yet somehow she was the one who made them all nervous.

"I want you to accept this," her father said, not meeting her eyes, but holding her hand between his as he spoke.

"Not near Christmas," she said in a panic. "I can't mix this with Christmas from now on." So they agreed to wait until she came home for spring break. While her friends made road trips to the beach for wet t-shirt contests and dollar Coronas, Sarah sat beside her mother on the hospital bed each day. Tilted toward upright, their bodies stretched and equal in length, Sarah watched the familiar body shut down. The nurses brought her a lunch tray just before noon, setting it down on the table that wheeled across the bed. It had been years since she ate pudding. She spent hours finishing three American novels for her seminar on Modernism and holding her mother's cold hand as the March winds blew against the window and brief moments of snow ricocheted past the glass.

* * *

As Sarah settled into the rhythm of traffic on 95 and they left Baltimore's skyline in the rearview mirror, she recalled the line of her mother's beating heart going flat. There was nothing else to the end, just an electronic sound shifting from a rhythm to a steady empty alarm. She kissed her mother's cheek before her own tears started, climbing off the bed as the nurses arrived to take over the room.

"I'm hungry," Franny said from the backseat.

"Ok. There's a rest stop not too far ahead."

"Is there pizza?"

"I think so."

"Can I get it or do I have to get a burger in the line Daddy likes?"

"What do you mean?"

"You know. Those places where we go and there are different choices, but Daddy only likes to wait in one line so we can get back in the car?"

"Any line you want," Sarah promised as she pulled off the highway. "And we'll eat inside." As she locked the car and took hold of Franny's hand, she looked at her watch. Some-where overhead Kyle was on a plane; he had been in the air for hours now, and she had not been worried about the flight. The lights of cars pulling in and out of the parking lot made her think of all the destinations linked to this highway and all the highways around the country, throughout the world. She could return to this car and drive anywhere she wanted to go. Such a thought never occurred to her before. For now, she would sit with Franny at their own table for two and eat, eventually rejoin-ing the stream of cars journeying together through the dark.

On the Ice

She climbed out of the pickup and her skate blades banged against her chest. Cold pressed at her cheeks, and the tall lights above the rink glowed through frost like the particles on her window in the morning. The door was heavy and hard to close with the thickness of her hands in double mittens.

"See you at 8:30," her father said between the small space where heat almost lived and then the bang of metal. He pulled away in his truck. Her boots crunched, and the noise moved up through her body and jaws. It was a short, uncertain walk across icy gravel to reach the skate room crouched between two rectangles of ice: The Town Rink. To her left she saw the swirl of hockey players, the crash of boys against boards and the puck she could never quite keep an eye on when she tried to watch them, especially Robbie, play. A whistle sounded over the noise of her boots and then the clacking of sticks and the scrabbling of blades as the bodies swept down the ice together. To her right, beneath a string of yellow lights that glowed weakly in the January sky, groups of skaters circled and wove, some fast and alone, others hand in hand; a long connected line of them swung by playing pop the tail. The lead skater stopped and forced the circle around a center until the final skater gained momentum and screamed while shooting out in a circle faster than anyone could skate alone. She had been that tail and felt the rattling of her teeth as she shot out like a bullet, trying to keep her legs in line and her feet beneath her.

In the shed she tightened her skates the best she could and looked up as two girls sauntered in whispering together; their skates chunked on the black mats that crisscrossed the room to keep the blades sharp. As they passed her, their bodies gave off cold, pressed it like a layer of skin out into the room. They were older, probably high school and did not notice her as they huddled in line for hot chocolate. But she was pretty sure she saw Debbie's green coat pass by the boards as she came in. It was important to her that someone moved with her in circles, to cut the cold and hold it between them as she waited. Hockey practice ended at eight, and she insisted her dad drop her off by a little after seven so she could be there, involved and on her own, skating not just waiting, when he finished. Her breath caught a little as she stood to test her ankles, see if she could possibly be straight enough. She wanted to look like a better skater than she was, wanted the grace of someone who has worn skates a long time, has moved across ice as if it were walking. In her mind she could feel it, could see the straight glide, the turning backwards and letting the wind of her own making shift her hair to the front, as it did Debbie's. In truth, to make herself move backwards, she had to be at a full stop and carefully step her feet, getting almost no glide and then a little pushing and wiggling of the hips to generate motion.

"You're getting it," Debbie told her each time and then skated off at her actual speed. She was a good friend, returning and returning, taking her by the hands to give her a sense of greater speed than Margaret could generate on her own. And so she worked at it, this new skill, important in this new town, in this new season called winter. The Florida girl in her wanted to stay huddled in her room in these cold months that shouldn't involve the outdoors. But she was in seventh grade and the thought of nights alone, stretching to spring because she could not skate, was a picture she would not accept. Her parents bought her the skates before she asked for them. Both of them grew up in this world of endless winter and seemed to love its glare and promise. They even showed up at the rink with her to teach her the first night, until she told them she would never go back unless they let her go alone.

She knew she was making progress when Robbie finally spoke to her; it was three weeks after she got her skates. In math class he paused near her desk and bent over just seconds before the bell rang and Mrs. Griffin settled them all for attendance. "I'll be around after practice tonight if you wanna skate." She nodded and then focused on the homework sheet in her folder, the pencil marks across her page appearing as the arcs and angles of blades on ice.

Begging her ankles to hold straight, she maneuvered herself out of the shed. The night's cold was a wall she had to push herself into. There would be a storm by morning the weatherman declared; the clouds above her, hiding the stars as she stepped toward the ice, seemed to agree. The green coat was not her friend Debbie, so she had to make her slow way around the rink alone, her arms outstretched to keep her balance, much younger kids slipping in and around her. It took five or six trips around the circle before she was warmed up and steady. The other skaters were the picture of how she wanted to look as she tried to imitate their ease. And then there were hands at her waist that spun her and sent her arms flailing. It was Robbie, set free early from practice; he was quick and bouncy in small circles around her. His blades moved like the knives of chefs, carving the ice with their silver speed. He made quick cuts and angles back to her, dropping her hand and then picking it up again as she pushed each skate forward and begged herself not to fall, not to look afraid of each swerve he made in her direction.

Lifting both of her hands, he shifted himself backwards and began to circle faster, pulling her with him. The bumps in the ice rattled her from her knees up through her shoulders, but she held on, stayed upright. They circled the ice again and again, Robbie swerving backwards in and out of other skaters, making her hair whip in the wind as she longed for it to do.

They were still moving nearly an hour later when the lights went out. She was ignoring the numbness in her toes, the sharp ache in her calves where the top of the skate cut in. Her hands were clenched in his through mittens so thick they could be holding wooden sticks. As the rink shut down and the skaters drifted off the ice, he guided her in a final circle, through the sudden black, and snowplowed in the far corner. Pulling her into the shadows, he pressed her against the wood. Across the ice she could see other small groups, darker than the night, huddled on the perimeter of the rink.

There was something else this ice had to teach her as it settled into its silence. Its cuts and tracks did not speak but contained the story of each night carved on a silent face. Her back leaned away from Robbie as he trapped her between the boards and his chest; she felt the urge to struggle, like a small animal caged by a pressure that could collapse even as it admired The blades of her skates shifted forward until she was slipping, but his hands were there, under her arms, to set her up straight again.

"Easy," he whispered as they resettled, his voice deeper than she ever noticed. She was afraid to breathe and afraid of falling, afraid of her own heart that battered at her ribs and her eyes that looked anyplace but into the face before her. Still holding her under the arms, he lowered his head toward hers. Their freezing lips touched and she drew in a surprised breath. The salt and sweet of bubble gum and long hours on the ice mingled on the rim of his mouth as they made warmth, a match striking flame and fear, kissing away the cold of a January night.

Grandpa Visits

Nights when the wind is strong and memories steam like cocoa, my grandfather appears to tell my son he loves him. I have seen him, a small gust, dart behind the curtain when I come in to check before bed. I pretend not to notice the smell of his pipe, the shade of plaid he leaves when he moves. He must have something important to tell, something antique and great grandfatherly, perhaps earned from the varnish and wood of his history, the many chairs and buffets he brought back from their own dead places in the barns and attics of the North Country. Last night for just a moment, he stood still and nodded in my direction. When I tell my mother she doesn't believe me. When I tell my husband he ignores me. But Grandpa is delivering a message, and I intend to find out what it is. There must be some way to trap a ghost, at least I assume the internet will know. And wiki teaches me in a few easy steps. I can even download an app that will detect the presence of his heat, not that I need that, and I am to listen for noises like the banging of items on a shelf. They do not mention pipe smoke or the fact that the space beside the window turns to shades of plaid while I watch. If he would just talk to me once, I would leave him alone to do his haunting.

My iPhone firmly in hand, I stare at the screen and wait. Dillon rolls toward the edge of his crib and his arm smacks the wooden slats. I jump, then check again to see if Grandpa's heat has entered the room. The screen is blank, but I feel the tail wind of a memory shift across my skin. He has come. What they say about the thermals on screen is only half correct. There is heat, but also the chill of his passing like a thick moment of fog and then beside the crib, Grandpa's jeans hanging low on his hips, the heavy work shirt tucked into his brown leather belt and the fisherman's cap on his head. He removes the hat and runs his fingers across the gray hair, sliding it into place. We could have been in his workshop or on the edge of his garden getting ready to plant tomatoes. Each moment of having watched him, followed him, helped him, floods toward me. There were hours when he taught me without speaking, let me trot like a new puppy just a few paces behind in all his work. He was rarely still, his knotted fingers holding a varnish brush, sand paper, shovel, hose or the wooden handles of his wheel barrel. As I grew older, I carried and settled the details of his chores. In just a decade, he aged and became a voice of directions and desires, needing me to put into practice the many hours I had only been a pair of eyes. He taught me how to work and how to pay attention.

Dillon can never have these moments. This barely visible presence and my stories are all he will have of this man who died within days of his birth. Only once did I place my son in Grandpa's arms, the hospital bed in his den, upright as he could barely lift his head or speak above a croaking whisper. I realize as I stand there just how much I miss him. In these months following his death, I have been busy with the details of being a mom and have wanted to forget the hospital death smell and papery skin, the horrible brown vomit and fevers he was too sick to hide. These memories do not sift through me and bring joy. I want him to visit me because this ghost does not resemble his final year; this ghost does not writhe in pain or throw bedpans at the wall; this ghost is not the dying grandfather I nursed, but the grandfather of my childhood, the grandfather of a past I want to relive, recapture, put on like a scuffed pair of boots that know the angles and knots of my feet. And then this grandfather, here now, reminds me he is still mine.

So I put away my phone and leave them, hoping my tiny baby will recall some grandfather relic passed to him in the shadows.

Cushioned

"Lehman Goes Under, Financial System Braces for Storm"
New York Times
September 15, 2008

"Nation's Financial Industry Gripped by Fear"
New York Times
September 15, 2008

Steve fell playing handball, nothing special, straight onto his left wrist and he would spend the next six weeks in a cast. The pain pills made the weekend cloudy, but by Monday the cast bit like a spiked collar on the edges of his forearm. Then an ache began, radiating slightly behind his thumb and moving outward with the pulse of a clock.

"Rest it on something, a blanket or pillow," the doctor told him, and Steve asked his wife to go to Target.

The blue piping around the pillow's edge captured his eye at once, a soft sheen that kissed his fingers as he held it. His blanket from childhood felt this way, rimmed in a shimmery satin. The pillow had a quilted face, puckered square sections split up by stitches and the fluted edge his fingers couldn't leave alone. When Steve placed his arm on top of the surface, the soft satin hit exactly on the spot where his forearm grew red and aggravated. He tucked it just inside the cast and achieved instant relief.

Within a few days he learned to prop it between the door handle and his left thigh when he drove, but put it begrudgingly in his briefcase when he walked from the parking garage to his office. The talk all morning had a nervous, uncertain hysteria, laughter too loud and glances too quick when colleagues passed in the halls or stood by elevators. It was impossible not to check and recheck numbers in accounts, look for something to do about it all, even as they hoped and waited for it to blow over. At the day's first meeting he left the pillow on his desk chair because he felt just the smallest twinge of embarrassment. He excused himself by signaling an important phone call coming in before Liam finished the most recent impact projections and analysis in light of the Lehman collapse. He sat the rest of the meeting out, his arm at ease and the city moving by around him, as he stared from the fourteenth floor.

"Doctor's orders," he claimed when he pulled it out at Mario's and set it beside the silverware.

"Landed like a crane," Dennis, his handball partner, assured everyone. Nods from colleagues conceded his injury.

That afternoon the pillow and his cast sat in full view on the conference table as Steve talked through his Power Point. The firm's partners accepted his request to sit during the presentation, forgiving him this noticeable weakness and maybe even listening a little more. Near the final slide, he saw Mr. Peters stretch his arms out and reach to caress his probably arthritic wrist as he stared at the pillow, no doubt admiring its smooth texture. By 4 p.m. they asked him to be lead consultant on the Conklin account, one of the largest for the firm's industrial management division.

"Of special significance now," Mr. Peters said.

Julie looked shocked the next night as they walked from the car to the restaurant to celebrate the new account. She wore a dress and lipstick. He watched her coming out of the shower before they left, saw her carefully apply lotion and put on diamond studs. But under the lights of the parking garage, she stopped walking.

"What's under your arm?"

"What?"

"There?"

"Doctor's orders. For the pain."

"You're kidding? Here?"

For a moment he almost told her about Peters and his longing, the look he caught across the table. But she tapped her foot, and he knew she wouldn't understand.

"You want to eat or not?"

"Not if you've got that thing on the table."

As they ordered their drinks, he stretched his fingers out beneath the tablecloth, reaching, but not liking the feel of his pant leg.

"Be right back," he told her as he stood up and placed his napkin on the chair.

In the men's room he rinsed a bit of water across his face. If he sprinted he could make it down the street and back before the calamari arrived. In the car he rested his arm for just a minute, the springy filling softening not only his wrist, but the very air in the car. He breathed in deeply and felt his chest relax from the top rib, down the sides of his waist, a warm, captured feeling like he was inside a sleeping bag and drifting slowly. He snapped his head up. Julie would be waiting. The urge to stuff the pillow inside his blazer almost overwhelmed him, but he shut the door and took off running.

"You're breathing hard," she said. A fork balanced in her hand, moved the fried pieces of octopus around on the plate. She stabbed one and dipped it in the plum-colored sauce. "And sweating."

"No." He shrugged, sitting down and picking up his fork. "This looks good."

She didn't say anything on the ride home when he placed the pillow on his left thigh before starting the car, but he knew by her silence and the way she stared out the side window, looking up at streetlights and the tops of buildings, that she was not speaking to him. He fell asleep on the couch during the eleven o'clock news, the pillow on his left hip. In his dream he was petting Penny, the Labrador retriever puppy he got when he was nine. She squirmed beneath his hand, her fur warm and gentle, then curled up on his lap and went to sleep as he caressed the velvet edge of her ear.

At the table the next morning, he rested his cast on the pillow and the paper across the top of his cast while he read about proposed school boundary changes and the possible site for a new strip mall, temporarily on hold. It became his habit to fold the paper away from the front page without reading anything. Taking a sip of coffee, he arched his back, feeling the night on the couch as it settled along his spine. The crinkling of a cereal box drew his attention, and he saw Julie at the counter in her spandex.

"A run or the gym?" He hoped they were now speaking to each other. She didn't answer, but came to the table and sat across from him.

"Pilates."

She pulled her hair into a high ponytail and removed all traces of last night's make-up. He always appreciated how well she took care of herself, how she could have been in her early thirties even though they both turned forty the year before. She never made a big deal out of dieting or exercise, but turned down desserts and went to the gym. It mattered in his business, at least a little, that he could show up at cocktail parties and the occasional work dinner with a slender, put-together wife. As he watched her eat her cereal he had a strong memory of her pregnant for their daughter Alyssa, how round and full she had been. They traveled to Saratoga Springs for horseracing late in her pregnancy. In a tiny room at a Victorian Inn, she flopped on the antique double bed, arms outspread, the hill of the baby rising off her belly, until one of the bed slats slipped. The whole mattress crashed to the floor, the headboard just missing her. As he pulled her from the wreckage and made sure she wasn't hurt, she had already started to giggle. "Shouldn't have had that last piece of cheesecake." But four months later, she was back in her old jeans and gotten even thinner in the last few years. Kind of gaunt, he thought as he looked at her hollowed spaces and the defined lines of her biceps. When he held her now she was all angles and bones, nothing soft or comfortable to relax on.

"Enjoy." He lifted his coffee toward her in a salute as he stood up from the table. Holding the edge of the pillow with the four fingers of his injured hand, he tucked it quickly between his cast and his hip, liking the way it filled the space and kept his arm from bouncing as he moved.

"What are you doing this morning?"

"Not sure." It would normally be a golf day for him, but he was still a few weeks from swinging a club. He hadn't longed for golf or handball since the cast. Instead he could feel himself stretching and reclining in the hours of nothing scheduled, like summer when he was a kid, the days open and slow. "We could go to the movies later."

"You hate the movies."

"Not always." He stood behind her with his good arm resting on her shoulder. "Isn't there something Alyssa wants to see?"

She stiffened, and he felt the heavy breath rise in her shoulders as she drew it in. "I know you went to the car last night. Don't even lie or think I get it. It's creepy how you carry it around, search for it when you've put it down." Her sigh was loud. "But it's only four more weeks."

Steve continued fingering the pillow as she spoke, playing across the texture like an instrument. Four weeks he heard her say, only four weeks. The cast would be off, the wrist healed.

"I have to go." Julie pecked him on the cheek, then the clatter of her bowl in the sink. The picture of his healed wrist continued to kick around in his mind; he stood for several minutes trying to catch his breath.

"The End of American Capitalism?"

The Washington Post,
October 10, 2008

In the month that followed he let Julie wash the pillow twice, and he did not take it in the shower with him. Otherwise, it was in his hand, the movement to pick it up when he rose from a chair or shift it to his hip as he walked, now completely unconscious. It was tucked neatly in place on the Friday afternoon that he pulled open the glass door to Dr. Tabor's office and gave the receptionist his name. In the waiting room, he leaned his head against the wall. His fingers automatically stroked the quilted texture. He often took these few moments to clear his head, to feel the breath in his body like he imagined in a yoga class. His mother came to mind, how she used to hold his head on her lap and run the tips of her fingers along his face, over the bridge of his nose, around the eyes. Her touch was gentle and smooth as he lay with his eyes closed, his face connected and tingling along the path her fingers made.

"Mr. Cantwell?" He heard his name, "Mr. Cantwell?" He opened his eyes. The black and white, Ansel Adams mountain came into focus on the office wall.

"Have it off in a jiffy," the nurse said as she led him to an examination room and thought he felt a twinge; maybe the bones weren't quite knitted together. He flinched when the doctor knocked and backed into the room pulling a metal cart that held a two foot long blue cast saw. On the end was a circular blade that made him think of junior high shop class. They shook, and then Steve felt his hand lifted from the pillow.

"Grip tightly," the doctor said. "Any pain?" Before he could answer, the doctor twisted the arm over and was pressing on the uncovered part of his palm. "Should be ready." He turned and picked up the saw. "Bet you'll be glad to have this gone."

The doctor placed the blade edge against the plaster at the base of Steve's middle finger; the saw whined as the blade reached a dizzying speed ready to slice off his entire forearm. It sounded like a wasp attack. Without thinking Steve flipped his left hand over and his fingers touched only the wool of his pants; it was just on his lap, where did it go in the last few seconds?

"Hold on. Stay still." The saw eased into neutral. Dr. Tabor gripped the cast again and flopped it over. "It won't cut you." Steve leaned over to look on the floor, his heart sped up; he could feel the surge of adrenaline as his temperature rose, his bowels shifted.

"Where'd it go?" His throat was tight and dry, the words barely able to claw their way out.

"This one?" The doctor leaned down and returned with the pillow in his hand; its blue color immediately settled him like a cool cloth on a feverish head. He placed it beneath the cast with his good hand, then closed his eyes as the back of his fingers came in contact with the fabric.

"Ready now?" He looked away as the crystallized, spinning blade chewed once more at the plaster. There was no way to soften this job, to ease into this loss. Minutes later he was still dazed as Dr. Tabor gave him his final instructions. He could only stare at the empty space around his wrist, feeling like an amputee.

An hour later he entered his house expecting a quiet Friday evening to finish his work, but found a crowd of girls dancing and flinging themselves around the family room. Julie agreed to host Alyssa's soccer party; he could just recall such a conversation. But before he could say hello to anyone, Alyssa pulled him into the front hallway for a family meeting, where she hissed and pointed at the pillow he still carried against his arm.

"It was bad enough when you had a cast."

"My wrist is fine. Thanks for asking."

"Mom." Her rolled eyes held such exasperation he wanted to smile.

Julie turned her toward the family room. "Back to the party."

"Ok. I'm ready." He expected her version of annoyance with him and resigned himself.

"She's fifteen. Your socks embarrass her," Julie said. This time he did smile. "It's weird, seeing you still holding it." She reached and grasped his wrist, the pillow dangled from the tips of his fingers as she inspected his arm, white, invalid skin where the cast had been.

"But you're different. It's before seven on a Friday night and you're home." She hesitated, almost started again, her fingers still running over the smooth length of his forearm. "Just wait out here for the pizza." She kissed him gently on the lips as she dropped his hand.

"Financial Crisis Suicide Numbers Mounting"

Huffington Post,
October 21, 2008

He put the last pieces of his presentation together over the weekend, continually testing his wrist's turning freedom, its motions easy and working. As he moved the final graphics into place, he rested against the puckered surface. It felt like massaging fingers, and he sighed with pleasure. But a quiet voice in his head commented on the need to hide the pillow, to be discreet, and he knew it spoke the truth. Yet it wasn't hurting anyone. Like a rabbit's foot or four leaf clover, it brought him luck, turned up the volume of success in his life, at a time when that should have been almost impossible.

The silence in the car soothed him. Steve never imagined how good it would feel to drive without listening to the news and traffic reports, but it became one of his new habits. He didn't plan to give it up. Grateful for the pillow resting beside him, he steered onto the beltway the morning of his final proposal to Conklin's representatives. He studied lists of employee names, flowcharts and workforce hierarchies; he knew the statistics and hard facts of how to make them leaner and more profitable. Brake lights. Traffic stopped completely. The dashboard clock showed plenty of time. The car in front of him crept forward, its lights signaling like Morse code. A hundred yards and he was beside the accident, a small sedan crumpled and pushed back almost to the windshield while a Hummer sat idling, unscathed and tank-like. The accident was only a few minutes old, no police, just men in suits by the open driver's side door. The face of the driver was cushioned against the airbag, her eyes open, but glazed, her cheek pressed against the soft explosion that protected her. One thin track of blood ran from her bottom lip to her chin. Traffic inched itself along, and he scanned the lanes to see if he could get out. At the next exit he saw a Target sign and pulled into the parking lot without thinking. Forty minutes later he stood before the men of Conklin Industries, his boss and assorted colleagues with a flash drive in his right hand and the pillow in his left.

"These are the hard numbers you came here for." He presented the flash drive. "Production and profits will increase. People will lose their jobs, their homes. You will make money." He nodded toward the head of the table. "Prosper by year's end." Raising his left arm and letting the pillow hang free, he panned around the room so they could all see. "Or you can go another way."

He walked around the table to the double door and called to the waiting interns who entered with Target shopping bags. He nodded around the room, and they began distributing the pillows. He had only taken the bright colors from the store shelves: red, gold, purple, preschool colors like blocks or finger paints.

"I want you all to close your eyes and remember the important, soft things in your life." Not one person in the room followed his instructions, but he continued. "For me, the best one is the way my daughter smelled after her bath when she was first born. I would rock her and put my nose right against her head." Every pillow sat untouched, and a few people began shifting paper. "I know how this sounds. Crazy. Like I need a long vacation." He pointed toward his boss and a few heads turned. "But if Conklin Industries can become one of the soft places for its employees, a place that cares about them, comforts them in this difficult time, you won't need to cut jobs because you'll have their loyalty. You will be something they want to protect." The door opened behind him; two of the security guards from the main lobby entered.

"There is a way to make this work." He was out of time, but still hoping they might understand. "You just have to give it a try." Placing the flash drive on the corner of the table, he backed his way out the open door. He stood still in the hallway, worked his fingers across the velvet and looked through the door as it swung closed. Spots of color stood out through the frosted glass, vivid and alive on the hard surface of the boardroom table. In the elevator he wondered how long they would be left there untouched, who would finally haul them away, take them to the dumpster in the back-parking lot.

Fifth Grade

One weekend **Kenny Lustyik and two friends** snuck off to explore the spring ice as it caromed its way down the swelling river. When the fire whistle blew, the town paused, waiting hard. Soon we knew- the two boys, Rob and Adam, their arms frozen to the hull of a canoe, screamed Kenny's name, even as the ambulance doors closed them in, and the siren stopped splashing red along the shore.

We stayed gathered at the bridge in the cold; his mother pressed tight to the metal, almost rocking over, until her husband placed his own aching body against hers. Waiting, two parent statues, icicle stiff, and then Kenny's body came free of the river, rose up from beneath an ice flow, pulled from the sticks and debris of winter, by the divers, who placed his rigid body in his mother's empty arms.

Kenny owned the snare drum. He could slide the drumsticks over his knuckles, then grab the ends, bringing our song to a close, almost like we were real musicians. Only he smiled during band. Rob, who played the trumpet, returned to school after a week. His eyes swollen, he walked in a bubble, clearing space at the lunch table and down the hall. He never told anyone how his mother slept with him, to make certain of his warmth and to wake him when the dreams began. He hated needing her there, but only she could make the picture of Kenny disappear- the swirling water, the hand reaching out, and Rob too frightened to reach for him as the hood of his sweatshirt, a shock of red, passed by. Adam stayed out of school for two weeks and didn't speak once he returned. He'd been a drummer like Kenny, but he went to the nurse rather than band for the rest of fifth grade. He couldn't tell any of us about lying awake in the tight rectangle of his bed as Kenny rose from beneath him, and they reached together for the canoe. But then a twist and spiral, the water sucking at them, a vacuum that would not stop and he

87

felt the pull on his legs, thought it was the current trying to drag him down; he kicked, hard, connected, hard and hauled himself up on the canoe. Closing his eyes, he breathed out the river and shock a little at a time. He never saw the red of Kenny's sweatshirt disappear. All night, breathless and sweaty, he called for no one.

For all of us, fifth grade is a deep pocket where Kenny's image remains. Through sixth grade and seventh, as Adam transferred to a new school and Rob kissed his first girlfriend, pressed against the splintered boards of the skating rink, we remembered Kenny. When we were seniors his mother begged us to put her son's picture in the yearbook and we complied, still remembering, but from a distance, and only for a moment when we opened to the page dedicated to his freckles and crooked front teeth.

Ice Dance

The snow began to fall north of Syracuse, the snow belt, the Pulaski exit where Lake Ontario meets the edge of the St. Lawrence, where 20 below zero is a familiar number in January. But this was mid-November and when Laine left her baby and her house, it had been nearly sixty degrees in central PA. More than five hours of driving up and through the devil's asshole, her husband's description of Route 81 north toward her home-town, and the weather was much less easy. Her parents didn't even live there anymore, so they hadn't been back since before she was pregnant with Luke, and if she listened to Jack, she wouldn't be on the road now. The sky promised heavier flakes soon, but these small, spitting bits were familiar, a place to put her attention, almost a comfort as she drove the long road alone.

Since the phone call the day before, she booked a room near the hospital, pumped thirty-six hours' worth of milk, and thrown a few clothes in her gym bag.

"What's this got to do with you?" Jack asked, stretched out on their bed while Luke grabbed at tufts of his beard.

"Allie said he asked for me. He hasn't said much since it happened."

"A five-hour drive because he said your name?"

"We were close once. I've known him my whole life."

"Which one is he again? They're all a blur from wed-dings." She laid her hairbrush down on the counter and joined him on the bed, her body stretched across the quilt, their son squashed between them, close and tight as she longed for them always to be.

"All we need is the cat now, a family in five square feet," he said and started to sit up.

"Don't." She placed a hand on his cheek, lifted just a bit under his chin until he couldn't shift his eyes away. "He was the one alone at the bar when Laurie got married. Kind of short, looks like a wrestler. A group of us pulled him on the dance floor and he sat down in his suit, crying. He tried to kill himself, and now he wants to see me. It's only a night."

He sighed and leaned in to kiss her on the forehead, his lips quick and careless like a drive-thru burger. And they left it alone. Jack was not the type to be jealous of her high school friends, so she suspected it was more about having to stay alone with Luke, a thing he never did for more than a few hours at a time. She dropped Luke at the babysitter the next morning and was on the road by 10. And there wasn't any cause for jealousy, for thoughts of Danny even. Yes, they knew each other since first grade, moved always in the circle of kids from their town, but it was a small town, their neighborhood a smaller piece of it. He was like a brother, no not that. They would have stayed in touch if the bond was that close. A cousin maybe, one she spent a lot of time with as a child, but then lost track of. College, their twenties. She could see him at various weddings, recall a few Facebook posts, and once he tried to organize a weekend of boating back in their hometown, an invitation to all of them via text. If she remembered correctly, he had been angry when nobody could make it.

Dark sure started fast and early this time of year. The road north through Fort Drum, Gouverneur, Canton, each place seeming smaller, more boarded up or simply left behind, haunted by promises left to rot through the seasons. But as the light faded, the snow stopped hitting her windshield; away from the lake the weather was clearing. Danny's sister, Allie texted her the address of the hospital's new annex, "just out of town." It was set back from the road with a winding snake of a drive-way. Out in front, a pond, with scattered benches, and as she parked and stood up to stretch her back after the drive, the last of the afternoon sun, fighting through the clouds, laid down a pearled path across the surface of the water. A straight line to heaven? She shook her head to make such thinking go away. All drive she had been picturing Danny, his laugh, the neigh-borhood football games on the edge of the Meacham's field, how they threw ears of corn at cars when they were bored and had to hide in the rattling stalks when brakes squealed and a driver got out yelling. He had been all over the calendar of her childhood, too many memories to count, a casual, but constant presence, everyone's class clown and in small moments, a darker edge she didn't let herself think about. The memory of Danny in the middle of the dance floor, sobbing into his suit was not the only time she sensed something wrong. One trip home for Christmas, soon after she was married, she ran into him at Morelli's, sitting alone at the bar on Friday night while she picked up pizza and wings. They hugged briefly, his arms lingering, the smell of beer strong, spoken a few sentences while she waited for her food and paid. She refused with apologies his insistence that she sit and have a beer with her. And his voice had gone dark quickly.

"Sure, sure, run on home to the family, the hubby." On the bar in front of him sat a stack of peeled Budweiser labels, a way to measure a Friday night while the colored lights and strands of tinsel sparkled around him. She hadn't brought him up to anyone at her parents' house, hadn't known what to say about how sad it made her to see him there alone on the Friday after Christmas. And in that sadness, the thought that she hadn't invited him home, hadn't included him in the evening of board games and drinks around the kitchen table with her family. He sounded mean, maybe bitter. Couldn't lonely sound just like that? The distance in years between them seemed more like an ocean than a stream they could cross toward shared memories. Yet here she was in the car, the suicide attempt compelling her to action of some kind. "I'm terrified he'll try again," Allie said. "He'll be out soon and alone in his house."

The wind whispered through leaves still clinging to their trees, and the emptiness held her still. Had she really grown up in a place this silent? And why had Danny chosen to stay?

The hush of the sick greeted her in the lobby. Floor three in the elevator: quiet shoes, soft overhead lights that shone on murals of the river, a pretending peace, and she spotted Allie in a glassed-in room, pacing and glancing around, a phone in her hand. They waved, Laine wondering how long it had been since they had seen each other, maybe high school graduation? She was two years younger than Danny, and Laine couldn't remember her at any of the high school weddings she attended. She looked like her mother, a woman who sometimes driven kids to the beach, her cigarette out the window, red nail polish, tinted hair cut to fall in slick waves around her face. Mrs. Wolensky was the cool mom singing to the radio and the first in their neighborhood to be divorced. Now here Allie was, looking just like her, the same intense stare and heavily lined eyes; she looked tough and confident, even with the crow's feet, tired lines around her mouth, and the distinct smell of cigarettes when they hugged.

Before Laine had a chance to ask anything or say she was sorry, Allie started down the hall and was pushing open a door, her voice suddenly bright and loud a few steps ahead.

"Look who's here! All the way from PA." It was a blur of expected hospital rooms as Laine stepped in, like a TV show with the tray and the metal bed, dim, shadowy light and a smell of too many cleaners, the plastic bags of fluids and meds hanging on hooks. The only thing missing was the sound of beeping, a sound Laine remembered from a visit to her grandfather when she was young; his heart, she had been told and the sense of a heart making such a sound remained in her mind. Allie stood on the far side of the room, shuffling a stack of papers and a plastic container on the tray pulled across the bed. She looked tired in the empty way of war survivors, a gray web of exhaustion, a habit of moving through days because there was no choice.

"Did you hear me Danny?" Her voice was loud and slow, like she spoke to a very deaf old person or a sulking child. She picked up the plastic container, a small pitcher with a straw sticking out and held it toward the body in the bed.

"Have some juice," she said as she bent down.

He sat up then, his body under a sheet shifting and rising, his shoulders covered in hospital print, white piping at his edges, like some sea animal surfacing in a net. His face had collapsed somehow compared to her memory, smaller, but also deeply lined like laundry needing an iron, scruffy too and no matter how she searched for him, she couldn't find the Danny she knew. Walking down a street she would have passed right by, nothing familiar.

"I don't want fucking apple juice. Jesus am I five?" And then she knew him, the voice made them all laugh in class, imitated the stutter and repeating of "essentially" that drove Mr. Jules the chemistry teacher out of school. There he was, and among all the expected but confusing hospital details, his voice sounded like a life jacket, a truth floating in the hours of her day, helping her know she was right to come.

"I'll leave you two to talk then." Allie tucked herself in with a breath and the pursing of her lips. This sister effort, supporter and cheerleader and juice purveyor was effort Laine suddenly realized would be forgotten or held against her forever.

Still believing in the sound of Danny's voice, the familiarity of it, Laine pulled up a chair and sat, ready for this visit now, ready for a chance to catch up.

"It's good to see you." As soon as the words left her mouth, she wanted them back, and she let her eyes rise toward the window, above his head, away from whatever waited there. The sun still played along the edges of the sky, a peeled back sort of sunset, understated and washed out, worn down by the chasing darkness. She knew she should look at him, see how her words *had* landed. His eyes were closed. Breaths slow and quiet, like he had fallen asleep as soon as Allie left, maybe the anger over the juice all the energy he had. Medication? Should she speak again? There were not instructions for such encounters, such moments, and Laine wondered if tiptoeing out of this chilly, shrouded room might be the right decision.

The group text between their high school friends started around after Allie told them in vague details that Danny had "made poor choices," "needed help and rest." They spent a few days replying all, wondering what happened to the funny guy they all knew, sending prayer emojis with bible quotes, and dispensing a little mean gossip about how he tried to end it, always careful to leave Allie off that thread. Laine read each one, sad for how quickly they could sound like high school kids again, mean streaks and frantic emotion. And Allie never shared more, so nobody knew what he had done. In the private texts and phone calls, the same vague mentions of trouble, even as she asked Laine to come visit. In spite of herself, watching him in the bed, his breath so easy, the minutes stretching, she found herself looking, trying to pick out any tell-tale signs. He had no visible symptoms, no wound or marks on his neck, nothing bandaged that she could tell, but his wrists were under the blanket. Hadn't she read somewhere men were usually violent, guns or hanging? She got up and looked around at the machines, inspected the newspapers and magazines, all without touching anything. Was there a chart somewhere with details?

Nothing changed as she moved more and more freely about the room, opened the closet to see a plastic bag of clothes, a pair of dirty Nikes, a black fleece coat hanging there. She reached down to look through his things, curious in a way she knew was wrong, but she couldn't quite stop the reaching of her hand.

"Anything interesting?" He was staring directly at her, fully awake now, his eyes clear and a bit of a smile, a half-smile that showed just the edge of his front teeth and took her back to who they had been. In senior English he jumped out the window one day after an envelope went around the room collecting money—if the pot reaches $20, I'll jump when the clock hits 3. And he had done it, his feet getting stuck on the way out, so he had to push himself off the brick of the outside wall, before clicking his heels and disappearing. He walked back into class minutes later with just that grin.

"Danny. Sorry. Just waiting…" she was helpless to explain, so she crossed back to the chair and stood behind it, forced herself to look at him.

"Allie called you."

She nodded, gripped the chair and wondered how long a visit was appropriate, then scolded herself for being such a coward. Impossible situations were not her thing, whatever made her think this was a good idea?

"She said you were asking for me."

"I wasn't." This time he looked away, and swallowed, stretched his neck like he was resettling on the pillows.

"Oh." A count started in her head, how long would she stand and stare at him. "Well I don't have to stay."

"Why didn't you let me go that day?"

"What day?" Again, words out of her mouth before she realized she was answering.

"You know." And she did. It had been almost on her mind during the drive, one of the memories she pushed away. She could see this now, standing in his hospital room, realizing with a jolt of physical truth that this man she didn't know, who had once been a boy she did know, had tried to kill himself, had actually wanted to die. The words had not communicated themselves to her until just then with the possibility that he might connect this act to her in some way. An image of Luke in his high-chair, cheerios like small life rings on the tray in front of him, his toothless smile. She shuddered with the clash of these two worlds.

"The ice dance," she answered at last, picturing each moment of the warm spring Saturday afternoon they hung out at the edge of the river's disappearing ice, the top of the dam where the ice floated and jammed up after rotting for days in the unexpected sun. It had just been goofing around, smoking a joint, watching pieces piled on top of each other and slowly, like movies of glaciers they had seen in school, a piece would break off and tumble over the edge, smash on the rocks below.

And then he jumped from the concrete ledge where they sat to the crystallized surface of the piling ice. "It's crazy thick," he said, standing still at first. And it was thick, but the sun had baked it for days, and yellow, rotted spots stood out across the surface, like bruises shifting color over time.

"Watch my Polish jig." He held his arms out, his face turned up to the sky and his feet starting a steady tap dance routine. He was carefree and silly, the perfect teenage way to embrace the afternoon and how good it felt to be outside and alive in early April sun. They were both grinning, laughing, and then he vanished. Laine could hear the ice collapsing, a giant whoosh and crack as the water rushing over the dam, only inches from them, was set free. On the concrete ledge, Danny's fingers, and she grabbed for him in the water, the cold piercing her hands like needles. She held him below the wrists and began to pull, just as his head surfaced. His body was sideways in the current, half of him already headed over the dam with the gushing force. She put her weight into heaving up, strained her thighs and launched herself backwards, all instinct and panic as she landed on her back. His body stretched out along the concrete too, all of him wet and twitching, as he gasped for air.

Remembering it in the hospital room, the moments as clear as a movie screen behind her eyes, she stopped. There wasn't any conversation she could recall, nothing beyond this moment of his body icy and beside her. Walking home later, his jeans froze in the wind and made a scratching noise, his legs artificially straight and stuck. And partway to their street, she took off her socks and put them on his hands, feeling the shaking, seeing the blue color of his lips. And she wrapped her jean jacket around his shoulders, wondered how he would ever get warm.

"Yeah. The ice dance. My shining moment."

She smiled at him, trying to believe they might now simply share this common memory, a reason he might think of her. Believe in this as long as possible, hold it.

"You probably think you saved me that day. Now you can remind me. Show me the light," he was almost shouting.

"I don't know."

"I don't know? I don't know?" He mocked her, tipping his head side to side and imitating a woman's voice, his lips pursed. "What kind of fucking answer is that?" He waited a beat as if she might try again. "News flash. Wrap your suburban empty head around the idea that I'd be happier not here. I've tried since that fucking day on the ice, but people show up, people like you, saving me." He began to flail his arms as he yelled at her, his biceps thin like dirty, collapsing snowbanks. His hair pasted to his skull and the corners of his mouth damp. She had never been this close to madness, to its temperature and pace.

"You all stop me because I'm so fortunate. Because I need a reminder of how lucky I am." He threw the bed's blankets back and began to swivel himself in the bed, like he meant to crawl toward her. She held onto the chair as she backed away; the legs clattered against the rolling table and for an instant they both watched the tumbling juice and magazine pages land on him.

"Fucking hell," he screamed as he swiped at the wet

mess on his lap. "Fuck you and your stupid mom judgements. I was cursing you. Saying your name to curse you. You should have let me go over. Your stupid superhero moment." He was panting by the time he stopped, his voice hoarse, but Laine sensed that he wasn't done. As he swept his arms again through the soaked chaos on his bed, the plastic pitcher finally clattered to the floor. Heat flared in her intestines. Sweat broke out along her hairline, on the back of her neck. Her mouth filled with a liquid she could barely swallow, and she knew she was moments from being sick.

"I shouldn't have come," she said. These words barely audible as she spoke them through the saliva she had to swallow. Getting away now the goal. She ran for the only door in the room that could be the bathroom, slamming it shut behind her.

Her face over the toilet, the violence of being sick took over. Moments later, as she wiped her mouth, she reached toward the sink and turned the water on, wondering if she was done. He wanted to die that day. It never occurred to her, and she refused to believe him now. The sound of his breathing on the concrete, the huge gulps of air were not disappointed, not angry. She clung to this memory, his breath. Life worth holding onto, always. In the mirror, her eyes were wet and sick looking, her face the gray of dirty towels. How could she go back into his room? Patting cool water below her eyes, carefully finding a breath, shuddery but slow, she gathered a sense of herself, small pieces to glue together. And in the space of the tiled bathroom, she paced a few circles.

If he wanted to die, if he always wanted to die was that an idea to respect? Her instant response was no, of course not. People were not supposed to choose death; they were supposed to choose getting help, fixing themselves. She was raised to believe everything was fixable. But his words made her feel small and not very bright, unable to grasp a truth he might have access to. She heard him like gongs in her head. He called her stupid? A mom? She looked at the rings on her hand, held up the symbol of her marriage success. He didn't have anyone, lonely. How sad? Was he jealous, not of her specifically, but what her life stood for? Perfect, perfect. The word she chanted to herself whenever the opposite threatened. What if she couldn't understand him, how he felt, what he wanted, couldn't let herself see it, but still he was right in some way? Maybe whatever made him suffer was bigger than any help available. A pounding began in her head, the pulse of her blood echoing as pain along her temples. The cold tile might be some relief, so she placed the right side of her head against the wall, held herself pressed to its surface, then turned to ease the left side. How had she ended up in a hospital bathroom with her temples against the wall? Enough.

In her purse she found Advil, shook out four and swallowed them with a cupped handful of water from the sink. She did not have an answer or even an idea as she fluffed her hair in the mirror and tried to adjust her sweater, prepare herself, and in the next moment, noticing the weight and pressure in her breasts. It was time to feed Luke. The pump was in the car; she imagined she would use it in the hotel after the visit to the hospital. But now she was trapped in a bathroom, afraid to go out the door, impossible but true.

There had to be a correct thing to say to him, of all the possible sentences she might speak. What did he really want from her? Luke needed her and Jack, back in the life she was constructing, people expected her. This was true, so she gripped the door, pulled it open with the words ready on her lips.

"I can't accept what you're saying." She forced the sentence out before reaching the bed. He didn't seem to have moved while she was gone. His eyes still wide awake, maybe a little crazier than before, like one of the guests on the Dr. Phil show who get themselves worked up enough to storm off the stage. He didn't look away, only glared a little deeper, still halfway on his knees like he might spring.

"Naturally." She had not usually been a recipient of his sarcasm. In fact, they had most often been the two laughing together at everyone else. He didn't see her that way anymore, an ally, cool enough to understand. It shocked her as she watched him, tried to think of a reply, how much she wanted him to give her credit, to believe she understood. He picked up the remote and began pressing buttons, staring into the corner where the TV hung. She felt dismissed as he shifted on the bed and resettled, attended to adjusting his position. The final wet papers and top blanket of the bed landed like a shovelful of dirt on the floor. The tightness in her breasts, the pulse and surge she needed to release was with her too, and she thought again of Luke, soon in his car seat in Jack's truck, then fed and bathed, his little wisp of hair damp while he drank his last bottle. Danny was not her problem. She wanted this thought to make her feel better.

"You weren't trying to go over the dam." She knew this visit was almost over; it was impossible for her to solve anything here. But maybe she could remind him a little. "You held on. I grabbed you, but your fingers were latched on that edge." He had not turned to look at her, but his hand lowered to the bed, stopped changing the channel.

"And I couldn't have lifted you out alone. No way." The memory played stronger in her mind now, the moment he broke free from the water, how she saw his legs almost over the dam, but then the huge push of him coming toward her. His legs had been in that push. It couldn't be any other way.

"Believe what you want and hate me for it." The ache in her breasts intensified again, but she stepped in toward him, delaying just a little longer. Her hands between the bed rails, resting on the damp sheet that covered him, she leaned in close, spoke directly to his profile, her voice steadier than it should have been. "You didn't want to die that day. I don't know about now, but not that day."

The words echoed in Laine's head, and she readied herself to continue speaking, to let words of any kind fill the space. Instead Danny turned his head slowly toward her, like the rotation of gears, one click at a time. She could not move, and in the suspended moment, she noticed a rim of green around his eyes and flecks through the light brown irises. They were locked in a child's contest, a stare too deep to break. There was time to wonder how long they could stay this still, what would break the silence, and finally was it safe to simply turn and walk out? Her grip loosened; she wiggled her toes. Without breaking his stare or changing anything about his face, Danny burst into laughter, aggressive, loud laughter, forced from whatever place in him lost all sense of humor. His mouth opened wide, the sound more like a bark than anything. She jumped as the noise and blast of hot breath hit her in the face.

Before she could reach the door, he began clapping as well. With her hands over her ears she burst out of the room, headed toward the elevators. Allie stepped in front of her partway down the hall.

"What is it?"

"He'll try again," she said without slackening her steps, their shoulders bumping roughly as Laine continued toward escape. She punched at the down arrow. Allie arrived beside her.

"What happened?"

"I don't even know," she said, feeling tears breach and begin to fall. The arrow lights shifted at last, the door a sweet parting of metal. Allie grabbed her arm as Laine stepped toward the opening.

"Please." It was desperate and filled with pain, a crack in the world Laine did not believe she could look at. Without much effort she could shake off Allie's hands, only touching her coat, two layers from her skin. Nothing demanded she stay here.

"It was pills," Allie said. "Two bottles and a fifth of vodka. The neighbor heard his dog barking or it would have worked." Alone in a house to make such a choice. And Allie's voice, the rust and squeak of the details so hard to share. Laine didn't want a part in this, didn't want to remember the boy who had been her friend, the house where they all played Monopoly and Battleship on rainy summer days, Mrs. Wolensky bringing them grilled cheese and Doritos before they knew they were hungry. Luke would have friends who came to the house someday, would know the basements and backyards of their neighborhood. The elevator door sat fully open, empty and lit inside, waiting for her. As it began to slide closed, she did not reach out to stop it. Turning away, she put her free arm around Allie's shoulders and began leading her to the waiting room. The tension in her breasts intensified, an itching, then a bit of release, the front of her shirt now wet. She would have to pump soon, but first, for the sake of who they all used to be, she would tell Allie the story of Danny's ice dance.

Stella Comforts the River

Stella carried her new lawn chair to the park and sat by the river. The water moved past. There was pigeon shit on rocks, a dead cat half buried in Purple Loosestrife, the gleaming, empty neck of a beer bottle, sharp as a wolf's teeth. Time passed and so did the river as she sat. Her brain hummed and clicked at its usual unhurried pace; no real way of telling the thoughts crossing there, but her heart pumped, her stomach digested. Eventually darkness settled; the wind carried small rain. The water was pockmarked and beaten.

So she waded into the current, her dress floating around her knees like a parasol and then collapsing, stuck to her body as she moved deeper into the swirl. She stayed in the current, stroking the surface and softly singing the songs of her childhood, while the moon collided with trees and the soft bones of the night commenced their clacking. At the end of her lullaby, she stepped one hint deeper and water closed around her. The moon alone looked upon the unmarred surface. On shore, winking back at the moon's face, sat an open, freshwater clamshell, like the pearled halves of an empty heart.

Unruly

On the night they met he led her to the dance floor, over the music, a clicking of her pointed heels, which she rarely wore and a thumping of her heart, which she rarely felt. Hands perfection on her and elbow turns of grace, he created a cave into which she could crawl. For this safety, she commanded her feet to follow, and it worked, hope glittering inches above the floor, for a time.

But her feet heard rhythm in a pattern all their own and forgot to pay attention when he led the way. As a couple they stumbled, bodies bumping, her feet perfectly in step to themselves. He smiled through her awkwardness, the willful assertion of appendages, and kept asking her to dance, until they were coupled and married and one.

Now they pretend her feet, like embarrassing family members, do not exist. He continues his smiling, sometimes: fists clenched, wanting to shake into submission, her unruly toes. And other times, the movements irritate too much, ring out a defiance he cannot help but attack. As much as possible, she silences them, locks them up and nails them to the floor. Their survival demands such measures to take away the wiggling, the beat she pretends not to hear. They shelter their lives from dancing. It is the only way. But still in night's hollow, bruised hours she wakes, with a scream at the entrance of her throat and sees in the moonlight, her feet, dancing beneath the comforter.

Trapped

In **late summer,** when the corn had ears growing fat and milky, she woke before the sun and jumped to the floor. She had slept in her shorts and t-shirt, sandals foot-ready beside the bed, her knife a heavy flop of weight in her pocket when she rolled from side to side.

The morning before she hung around the edge of the garden, trying to help her father empty the rat traps he set to catch the crows. He ignored her mostly as he carried the traps from the corn to the burn barrel, where the black promise of soil met their yard. One wood and metal device held only some feathers, an unfortunate escape, but in others, the dead birds were sliced nearly in two at the neck, dying with their eyes open to the sky.

Standing on tiptoes to look while he pulled back the quick metal bar and released the captured prize, she saw a flutter of white clouds reflected in the depth of one eye. A soft slide of feathers crossed her hand, and she pictured the wings lifting, the careless rise of feet off the ground, a pledge of air she longed to inhale.

"Can I have the eye?" she asked. Her knife, always in the pocket of her shorts, was ready to carve out the black hope of this death, the opportunity presented and in reach.

"Get in the house." He didn't look at her as he spoke. "No place for a girl." Tossing the dead body into the burn barrel, he started around the garden to the next trap, canceling the magic she longed to possess. Jodie watched his stride, his angled heels in the boots he always wore, grounded and stuck, a part of the earth even as he stepped. In the barrel, the feathers hissed as she slipped her knife back in her pocket. It should be her place, a girl's place, just as surely as it was his, she thought as she stepped lightly across the grass and closer to the house, where she would watch and wait for another chance.

Now she moved through the yard in the silhouette light of pre-dawn and settled herself on the edge of the garden where the churned earth was cool with dew and night remnants. The rows of corn with their sawing green leaves shielded her from the house. In the air above, the crows circled; their shadowed air and beauty made her long to fidget, to leap and join them, but she held herself down, rooted and waiting. They lowered themselves, and she struggled to keep her eyes on them in the gloom, until a smack and flutter echoed, followed by another. Her breath caught as she rose and gained her footing in the loose earth. A few strides and she was in the middle of the patch, the leaves rough and slicing against her face and arms as she searched in the gray light of sunrise for his traps. She moved with her blade open; it was important, she knew without thinking, to reach the bird quickly. The eye must still contain its light and sky, like the one she saw the day before.

She almost stumbled over the first body. The trap severed the neck. With her toe she nudged it, anxious about its size; for here in the corn and the dark, alone, it was larger than she expected. Nothing moved, and she bent over to squint at the head, searching for the magic of the eye, its power so close, its talent now useless. No gleam of sky reflected back as she poked. She stepped deeper into the rows, a cry from above and a quieter one to her right. Following the sound, she reached the next trap and could see the twisting of a body, a lifted wing circling and stuck in place because her father staked the traps to the ground. Morning light edged toward peach, a glow that fell on the black feathers before her and made them shimmer like jewels in a chest. Her plan had not accounted for a bird still alive; she could see its small chest pulse and the good wing beat uselessly on the ground as she drew close. The eye swiveled toward her as she looked down through the web of stalks. It took her in; she felt the seeing and then opened to the exact possibility of morning sky. She wanted this for her own, for the treasure of possessing it, the hope it filled in her with its infinite assurance of flight among the clouds.

Without thinking, she slammed her foot down on the space between its turning head and body. The beak reached once in her direction; she felt the brush of feathers at her ankle and almost leapt back, but the eye had shown her too much. She would have it. Increasing the pressure in her foot, she bore down, twisting against the neck until the head slumped. In the dirt, she knelt and readied her knife as the body settled into death. The head was soft in her hand. She touched the point to the eye's edge and carved around the space of the socket. The blade pushed below the surface to pop out the marble possibility. It landed in her palm, sticky and lighter than she expected, but rolling. She held it close, waiting. Across its bottomless dome, the clouds appeared. A cheer rose in her throat, and then the bang of her back door. She froze and hunched low, even though the corn hid her.

He came to empty the traps, and his whistling reached her ears. She could creep to the bottom of the corn, edge herself out and along the back of the garden, but there was so much open space to cover, past the low green of beans and carrots and potatoes. He would see her. There wasn't even time to choose an action as he rustled in and began his circuit of the traps. Two rows away, he paused, and she heard the metal snap as he opened, then released, the dead bird. His boots appeared moments later. Readying herself for discovery, she held tight to the tiny orb and looked up. The crows circled above her still, slow and unafraid, calling, basking, free of the ground and biding their time. He could never get them all, no matter how many mornings he emptied their bodies into his barrel. This was their real secret. The cry began deep in her lungs and blocked out the startled sound of her name. Squeezing her legs together, she lifted her arms and called again, willed her feet off the ground. Her flip flops slipped from her toes, and she felt his rough fingers on her foot, almost pulling her back, but she flapped once more, and her head burst out of the corn, soared into the gathering of black wings. The sky pressed close enough to embrace her as she rose and received this new height.

Verbs in My Sentences

The third time **Maggie left her husband,** she took the dog, but not the cat. She was back in four days with the fury tamped down in her gut and the guilt still a metronome in her head. Simon sorted every shelf in the apartment while she was gone and put every knife from the kitchen in a Tupperware container in the freezer.

"I knew you'd be back."

She had not told anyone she was going, so the failure to stay gone did not chime with criticism through her network of family and friends. In truth, the last few years she avoided saying much of anything to them because she knew how they waited for her to "come to her senses." Her mother sent rosary cards and pictures of St. Jude, Patron Saint of Hopeless Causes, which didn't make much sense to Maggie; if she was really hopeless, why bother? But her devoutly Catholic mother praying for a daughter to divorce her husband of nine years was not exactly in line with Maggie's childhood memories of her mother's doctrine, so perhaps looking for sense was not the point.

The cat dishes, normally squatting beside the dog dishes on a corner of the linoleum near the kitchen table, were gone.

"Where'd Betsy's dishes go?" The duffel bag she packed on Thursday night still hung off her shoulder while she dug in it looking for the dog's things.

"Out," Simon said, his head deep in the pantry where he was finding the makings of dinner to celebrate her return. She suspected he threw most of their food away, as he often did during a cleaning binge. Once he emptied her entire underwear drawer while she was at work because he found threads loose on a pair of her panties and one bra with a broken underwire.

"As in outside?" They lived on the third floor of a Victorian in a neighborhood of Boston that had once been respectable. Outside was a small weedy lawn and a rocky cliff that ended with a long drop to the expressway.

"She took off on me, but she'll be back now that you're home." He stood up and faced her, shaking a full box of gluten free shells and smiling with all his teeth showing, an expression that emphasized the pudginess of his cheeks. The medicine kept all emotions away from his eyes, and she came to appreciate that flatness like it was a calm lake on which her days might float without capsizing. The pasta had to be acknowledged and the cat forgotten if the evening had any chance of continuing.

The metal dishes clunked to the floor and Paul Revere, their Collie Lab mix, trotted to her side. She patted his head and lowered her bag, before getting him water. The porcelain of the sink gleamed at her when she turned on the faucet. As water filled the bowl, her wrist began to ache with fatigue, and then the dish slipped from her grasp and clattered into the sink.

"Jesus Fucking Christ," Simon screamed. He was beside her, pushing her out of the way as he reached beneath the sink for the paper towels and began mopping up the water, most of which had gone down the drain.

"Betsy doesn't go outside," she said as she left the kitchen and his obsessive wiping. He would be well over an hour searching for every drop. After locking her bedroom door behind her, she fell across her quilt in a dead man's float, her face buried where the rich, flowered scent of their fabric softener entered her nose. He washed all her bedding, a project deep down the list of things to do. It had only been four days, so if all the shelves and the bedding in both their bedrooms had been taken care of, he had probably not slept. Their apartment from the outside must have been a brilliant lantern through the hours of night, throbbing with his music and ablaze with light while his frantic cleaning made him a blurred silhouette whenever he passed by a window. She pulled into their driveway under these conditions before, when all the other houses on the street had settled themselves to a normal dark.

With a sigh she pushed herself off the top of the bed and swung to sitting cross-legged. From her bag she pulled her computer and the folders for work. It was so simple to fall into the numbers and details on screen, to let herself get lost in the straight columns of her job. Eventually she moved to personal emails, since she avoided them while she was away. Skimming quickly, she checked a box for deletion beside all the Groupons and Travelocity messages, the credit card options and weekend sales. Within minutes she reduced the unopened list to six emails, two from her college alumni association about an upcoming gathering at a Bruins game, one a happy hour invitation from a work acquaintance that she already missed and three from her sister-in-law, Carol who was a high school guidance counselor and tried to be Maggie's counselor, sending constant advice and articles about living with mental illness. Simon hated hockey. She clicked the delete box for the first email, but paused with her mouse positioned at the second.

During her four days away, she chose restaurants to eat in without considering the cleanliness of the silverware or running a check on recent health code violations. In a small town in the Berkshires she simply walked into a café and ordered macaroni and cheese that came loaded with lobster and a touch of cayenne pepper. Seafood, dairy, spice without thought or consequence, without guilt or judgement. Each time she left Simon, she imagined she would stay away, but after a few days, it felt more like a brief vacation that relaxed her enough to go back for another round of medicine, doctor visits, tracking symptoms and research on the internet. Her job required only occasional visits to the office or coffee with potential clients as she showed them their website options and explained her marketing strategies. This left her hours of time to be with Simon or think of reasons to be away from him. It was an exhausting charade. She moved to the next email without deleting the second hockey game notification. Immediately a video began to play and the folksy, fake voice of Dr. Phil spilled out of her speakers. Her sister-in-law was at it again.

She stared at the video without meaning to see it, her finger poised to close it, but hearing instead, "I can't imagine why anyone would choose to be with someone who makes them feel worse." He patted the woman's knee as he handed her a handkerchief from his pocket. "You need to ask yourself if you feel better when he's around or when he's gone. I'll let Casey think about that while we go to break, and then I'll come back and put some verbs in my sentences to let you all know what I think she ought to do."

Maggie watched the video three more times, never reaching the verbs in the sentences, but hearing the simplicity of feeling better. Railroad Street Café, the name of the restaurant where she ate and after the macaroni and cheese, an apple crisp with cinnamon ice cream. Simon could only eat or look at vanilla or chocolate—plain without any chunks or different colors and only if he remembered his probiotics and lactose pills. Usually she just skipped dessert in the interest of certainty and peace. When had time with Simon made her feel better?

Paul Revere scratched at the door and she climbed off the bed to let him in. He curled on the carpet with three turns of his body and she laughed, not for the first time, about the irony of acceptable, obsessive dog rituals. Something white stuck out of his collar as he lay in a tucked-up ball.

Dearest Maggie: I am sorry about the water, about so many things. Please come down and eat.

She knew dinner would be on the table, maybe with candles because he considered the details that made her smile. He meant to make her happy; she could never doubt that. And yet, she could imagine as well the six shakes of salt across his food and the tense moments while he tried to put the shaker back in exact line with its mate on the table. There could be no eating while he adjusted, so often their food was cold before the ceramic turtle shakers were back in their spots. *Someone who makes you feel better.* Could there be a day when coming home was something to look forward to?

Moving down the hallways, she paused to read the noises. He was muttering, but not loudly, and a cupboard door closed without banging. There was a rattle like a pan shifting off the stove and then the familiar pull of the refrigerator door. His back was to her as he placed a bowl on the table, so when he turned and saw her, his body jerked in a startle response. Then he smiled quickly.

"You came down." He took her by the elbow and guided her to her seat. A whispery, challenging voice in her head suggested she try to sit in the chair across from Simon instead of beside him on the right where she always sat, but she ignored it and let him settle her at the table. The bowl was filled with pasta and a brown sauce that looked like gravy, but was probably mostly soy, one of the flavors he trusted. Water was better for digestion without ice; she took a sip, missing the smack of cold she enjoyed the last few days. The salt and pepper shakers were not on the table, perhaps a change he was navigating. Reaching over her shoulder, Simon placed a platter of meat, thin slices, also covered in the brown sauce, next to the pasta.

"A little grace?" He reached for her hand and she flinched when the hot smooth fingers grasped hers. For some reason the blessing before the meal stayed with him from child-hood, even though like Maggie, he abandoned all other pieces of religion.

When he finished giving thanks and released her hand, he began spooning food onto her plate, counting the noodles as they fell. He stopped at twenty-seven and looked at her, his eyes still empty as a moonlit lake, then his hand shook, and he dumped what was left on the spoon in one quick motion.

"I'm sorry," he said, beginning to spoon meat onto her plate.

"I know." It would have been the moment she consoled him; all their relationship she made these habits okay by smiling her way through them, allowing them because they weren't really *so bad*. It became impossible to get a read on normal, to find the surface of the water from the dark, cloying space below. But glimpses came through. Each weekend away made the time with Simon unfamiliar at first, unwanted even as she settled herself to tread across the water of his illness once again.

"What's the meat?" she asked, her knife just beginning its first slice.

"Try it first."

She paused with her fork speared into the flesh. Some-thing in his voice, an edge she had not ever heard. On his plate the meat sat to the side, not touching the noodles as always, and she moved her gaze from his fork, just capturing some noodles, to his face, a gaze waiting for her.

"Something new?"

"Sort of." In his shrug she thought she sensed him poised on an edge. Something was at stake here, and he didn't want her to know. As she lifted the bite toward her mouth she kept her eyes on him. Did he lean in? Anticipate? It came to her in a rush, making her throw the fork on the table and leap up.

"You didn't?"

"What're you talking about?"

She was raving now, an image of Simon at the sink with the skinned body of their beautiful cat Betsy Ross firmly in her mind. He finally tipped in the direction her family continually warned her about. It explained so much, the knives, the water in the sink, the effort to set the table differently. She ran to her room and snatched the computer bag from the floor, stuffing her laptop in and pausing at her dresser to stow a few other pairs of underwear. It didn't matter really what she brought. She could buy new things; she just needed to get out. He was in the doorway when she turned to leave.

"Maggie?" He wasn't blocking her exactly, not that she couldn't push him away if she needed to. His lack of physical strength had always been part of his appeal, his need to be cared for, his body so unlike her father's.

"Get out of the way Simon."

"What are you doing?"

"Leaving."

"You just got back."

"You just served me our dead cat for dinner." She shouldered past him and he folded against the doorframe, barely letting her touch him.

"That's what you think? After all these years you could think that?" His voice, though soft, cut into her ears as she moved away. She slowed, then straightened and turned, realizing both what he said and the impossibly helpless voice, so Simon, so frustrating, but also so true. He didn't lie to her, and she learned to cling to his honesty as the best thing between them. Leaving was the right decision, but looking at him, wounded and struggling, she couldn't be sure. He finished sinking to the floor as she watched. When he looked up at her, tears formed in the corners of his eyes.

She had to lean toward him when he spoke this time, his lips barely moving. "We are worse than I ever thought. I'm worse. You should go. Nothing can fix this if you think I would really do something to Betsy."

It almost worked. Pushing her away for her own good brought her back more times than she could count. Without thinking she took a step back down the hall toward him, felt herself pulled into his orbit and the words that would sooth him, the apology and acknowledgement of her misunderstanding. As if from outside her body she could picture how she would be sitting in just moments, his head cradled in her lap as they each outdid one another with concessions and relief. He would need her there, so utterly and without question. His gratitude felt always like the greatest prize at the fair, the jackpot and for a few hours, maybe even a few days if she was lucky, they would tiptoe around together, careful not to stir up any dust or emotion, any conversation or desire to upset their happiness. But then another voice pushed into her mind. "Do you feel better?" It was Dr. Phil and the verbs she never actually heard. Stop was a verb and so was leave. No was not a verb, but she said it anyway, not shouting, but firm as her voice carried to the crumpled figure of her husband in the hallway.

"Not anymore," she added. Whistling to the dog, she picked up speed as she entered the kitchen, stuffed her keys in her pocket and let the fresh water in the bowl spill all over the linoleum as she lifted it from the floor and dumped it in the sink. She could stop for a sandwich and a new bag of dogfood at the grocery store. The beach was only a few hours away, Cape Cod and the feel of sand between her toes. Driving out of their neighborhood and out into traffic, out into the world where all the dangerous, anti-Simon things lived, she let her shoulders relax, her hands grip the wheel with instinct and pleasure. This was where she suddenly wanted to be, the only place she could be. Her phone rang, syncing through the car speakers. Simon's number appeared in the console.

"What do you say boy? Wanna go to the beach?" The dog turned his face from the window and then curled himself up on the front seat. Maggie gave the car some gas and then slid a finger to the "end" button, disconnecting the call.

Saying Goodbye

She rode on her bike with the smile of a child, and everyone knew she was crazy. Standing at the mouth of my father's
grave in the first heat of spring sunshine, I had been counting
the people at his funeral when Maggie soared into view with lifted legs, no underwear and a worn cotton dress tenting over the
bike's handlebars. Around her neck hung a grain sack from which
she grabbed handfuls of dandelion tops and flung them up in
the air, letting them arc around her. They fell behind, around,
without noise like soft yellow rain on already damp earth. She
circled nearer. The small twitches and coughs of the crowd grew
more uncomfortable. Townspeople shook their heads and avert-
ed their eyes in a common gesture; many witnessed such before.
Aunt Carol covered her face with her hands while Uncle Pete
put his arm around her shoulder and began whispering in her
ear. Several of father's colleagues from out of the area dropped
their jaws and forgot not to stare at the wild-haired woman who
wheeled under the elms like a mad circus performer, tossing,
flinging her gift to our father amidst the fender rattling of the
old bike. I had not seen my older sister in fifteen years. Perhaps I
alone caught, but did not honor, the flashing rapture in her eyes
as she said her goodbyes in spite of us.

There was joy in her shoulders thrown back as she prepared to bellow out the raucous laugh which finally silenced the
minister and turned every eye to her performance.

"Bye byeeeee Daddy," followed her braying: little girl
words in a forty-year old's voice. She screamed, near us now,
only bike lengths away and reached again into her sack. Showered with the pattering of yellow, I rotated at her speed, our
father's casket the epicenter of our circle. We orbited. Maggie
the rightful heir, the one who stayed behind and I, the prod-
igal, gone all these years and now welcomed. She would not
be enclosed or included here by anyone, although I knew she
deserved it more than us all, and certainly more than I who es-

caped and then avoided the years of struggle and illness in my family.

Partway through our circle of staring, I caught and held her eyes: a moment of undeniable knowing, brief as a sizzling match. Her weight rose on her toes, shoulders loose in their joints as she wobbled but balanced, upright like a bottle, set rocking and slowly tilting back to center. She knew mastery, staring at me, certain on the bike and unbending. Her hands stood out against the rusted turn of the handlebars. The same hands braided my hair, washed my clothes, played the flute at night by my bedside, caressing lullabyes from the old metal. She had been there always to shut out the scraping of night things, the terror of our mother's illness, the silence into which the house dropped. There had been Maggie moving us through the seasons with meals and holidays, songs and the lifting of our father's spirits when getting him out of bed was nearly impossible. Her hands had always been familiar to work, creased with the burns of an iron, the weeds pulled from our endless garden, but cleaned and rubbed with lotion each night through her teenage years to protect their appearance. Now they were almost black with dirt, a laborer's hands with no nails or flesh in view. "Maggie remains about the same." I could still hear from the letters over the years. He never let me see her like this, and I never tried to see underneath, let his lies comfort me, assuage my guilt and keep me away.

"Bye byeeeee," she called again.

We had all tightened and huddled; cattle-like we tried to shut out this enemy, this foreign presence. But in spite of myself I saw a moment of the sister I remembered. I knew almost nothing about her anymore, but she belonged here, had a place among us. I stepped from the tightness of the group, away from the edge of my father's farewell.

"Maggie." She rocked backward, braking and coming to a stop. My uncle's hands reached my arms and tried to maneuver me back where I had been, but I pulled away and stepped toward her again.

"Maggie." We stared each other down, and I nodded, could hear the shifting uncertainty behind me, but didn't care.

"Come here and say goodbye." I held out my clean, shaking hand as she got slowly off the bike.

Burning the Recyclables

She could add his clothes to the fire, his books, his video games. No, she should add them. That fit better. To stand in this freezing cold, her feet in untied boots and watch the newspapers and pizza boxes turn to thin, disintegrating ash and then float on the wave of smoke into the air, makes it seem possible and even powerful. She can picture the golf shirts in a smolder and then the bleed of colors as the flames pick and clean their vulture's way through his things. Would she even tell him if he asks?

Inside her son watches television, something Disney, but without a princess, while she stands in the December snow and lets the heat push her rage and fear from the surface of her skin. She will stay here, burning their week of paper trash and imagining her husband's belongings, until she can move again through the details of the day with the knowledge that he has left her. Their town is small; she will have to see him at the grocery store, China Wok where she loves the lo mein; his car will sit less than three miles down the road, in the gravel driveway of the house where he has moved with his new girlfriend. The situation is a cliché, and she does not know how to break free of this. With his gym bag and laptop, he stood at the door and hugged their son goodbye. Somehow this leaving was an option for him, a box on the application of their lives that she imagined was filled in and permanent. They agreed to certain terms. The wedding and the pictures confirmed this; the toddler years with Evan still confirmed this, but somehow, when she was not looking, not tracking him, not worried, he let himself drift into a new life, like the shift in wind that now blows smoke in her face. He was once here and now he isn't.

"I don't know what you want me to say." And he would not meet her eyes, this man who lived beside her for almost a decade. Because he heard on the radio that men who kissed their

117

wives before work had a statistically proven life span four years longer than men who didn't, they kissed goodbye at this very door every work morning as he carried his coffee mug to the car. Would that work with new girlfriends? Would it overpower the curse she chanted in her head for the last four hours? Would he think about it come Monday morning? She squeezes back the tears, scoops up a handful of snow and scrubs it across her cheeks, liking the sudden jolt of ice to her system. A few stray envelopes into the fire pit and she stands back.

The flames chew and crackle, but then relax as the final edges of cardboard collapse into black powder, small embers shrinking as she watches. The plastic container sits empty now, but the fire is not done. She will check on Evan, maybe bring him out to play in the inch of new snow. Moving toward the back porch and the stairs to the kitchen, her boots mark a path she will follow when she returns with the first armload.

Soil

It **was almost full dark** when Caroline looked up from her feet and around at the lettuce field she had been moving through. When she stepped off the road a few minutes ago, the harvesting trucks were in the distance. Now just in front of her, only a hundred feet away, a truck larger than a pick-up with wooden slats for sides, moved slowly down the row in which she walked. She heard the dusty footfalls of men near the end of their workday as they shuffled along on either side of the truck; the sheen of their knives was barely visible, a silver flash in the small space of moon, like the snapping of a photo, then dark again and the smack of a lettuce head dropped on the pile. Watching the silhouette of their movements, the space of their bodies a slight twist darker than the night, she thought of a puppet show, marionettes on the strings of God. And then she tripped.

The ground was before her, the smell of earth like raw meat by the time the pain in her ankle registered. She did not cry out, but patted the ground around her in a circle, searching for whatever made her fall. It was cool and round, ridged as she grasped it with her fingers, pulled herself to sitting and then cradled it in her arms. Iceberg lettuce, the size of a baby's head. Brushing the dirt away, she worked her careful fingers along each wrinkle until she found the stem where it once connected to the ground, to its roots, to the earth.

He was not coming after her. The tears no longer mattered, and she did not try to control them or even notice them as they blurred her vision, and she sat rocking in the middle of the field. It would only take him a few minutes to stow his things. While she was too far away to hear the slam of his trunk, she imagined it and followed the noise with the red certainty of taillights. Would he glance in the rear-view mirror? Was she worth that much at least, a final thought for the four years they shared? Being left was a thing she knew, a familiar pulse and then one side of the bed intact, a stillness that led to more time in her head than she liked. She would begin to eat, once the first days of paralysis moved away, tomato soup while standing at the stove or tuna fish straight from the can; no more evening meals of baked chicken and steamed broccoli, no more vegetables at all as she couldn't ever eat enough to make the preparation seem worthwhile.

It had only been two days since she told him, and he said, "Take care of it."

Standing at the sink, her hands loose in the steaming dishwater, she had not known she would accuse him. It never happened before. "You could at least be there."

When he stood, he hadn't looked in her direction. Instead he slowly rolled down each sleeve and rebuttoned the cuffs of his work shirt, with precision and luxury, like a surgeon. She read Allen on the patch sewn to his pocket, right below Jiffylube, and remembered hanging all five of his shirts Sunday morning, on the line he rigged between the back step and the corner of the garage. Her grandmother tried to teach her the importance of hanging a "good wash." It was essential to match socks, colors gathered near one another, all dishcloths together. Caroline had never given such things her attention, tossing the wet mess of shirts across the rope and moving on, assuming she brought other talents, other precision to relationships. But she knew her grandmother, dead now almost ten years, would have disagreed. After so many missteps, so many leavings and unmoorings, maybe she should have paid more attention, could go back now and fix this sort of shortcoming.

Allen returned after two and did not step down the hall to their room where she was awake and unsure if it felt better with him again in the house. In the morning she found hundred-dollar bills on the table without a note; he knew she would follow through, end it like she had two times before. But they were on the table that evening when he returned, expecting dinner, like always.

"I thought I made myself clear."

She pushed the refrigerator door closed, held the handle with both hands before she turned to him.

"You did. I just can't." If he had lunged, she would have known how to react, but he walked around the table like he was coming to hug her or catch her for dance steps as he had done so many nights of their time together. When his hands reached her throat and she felt her head hit the refrigerator door, it was a surprise. The calluses on his palms scratched the skin of her neck. She could see lines of tension across his forehead, down the sides of his mouth, but his eyes were glassed, distant, just how he looked when they made love. Her knee to his groin gathered in her as she searched his eyes for something she knew in the deep puddle of emptiness. He went down with just a small scream. And she ran. Two steps away she heard the noise of the hamburgers she had been frying and stopped to reach back and click off the burner. He was still on the linoleum, huddled around himself and moaning with a quiet, steady cadence. She ran to the lettuce field, the smell of wet earth and all those small, growing heads of green.

Now the dirt felt cool to her fingers as she dug into its thick, royal composition, its stillness and trust. She shifted onto her knees, urgent, afraid to stop; she flung the clumps behind her, then placed the head of lettuce in the hole her hands had made. She scrambled dirt up and around it, mounding, desperate. A clunk of metal, movement and the creak of wheels sounded on her left. Voices too, urgent now, calling near the end of the row. With a sputter, then steady swoosh, the sprinkler kicked on. Water tapped down rows, roving over leaves not yet ready to harvest. The lights of the truck blinked again, the brake released, the men continued down the row in the dark she would have to pull herself through.

Mercy

"I got a cooler in back, we'll stand there and get to it. You won't believe how easy this'll be," Marty said to Pete.

"So who drives? I don't wanna be stuck in here with you havin' all the fun."

"Why'd we bring Jill? She drives your tractor don't she?"

At the mention of her name, Jill looked at her father, not quite clear about what was being decided for her. She was eleven, not old enough to drive, not even old enough to be excited about driving. They turned off the pavement onto old railroad tracks, the rails rusty in patches and shining a little in other spots from the snow that melted overnight. Jill thought she knew this section of track from berry picking in the summer, but it was hard to tell when she rode around with her father on these outings. Every season looked different, and he knew so many places, all the places it seemed in their whole county.

"Guess it'll be ok. Your first driving lesson."

It did not occur to Jill to protest this suggestion because she loved trailing after her father through the light and the trees, along the near hidden trails of the forests he knew, his authority commanding the woods to yield its inhabitants. As the second child and second daughter in a finished family destined always to remain without brothers and more importantly, without sons, dressing her in a green and black plaid hunting jacket and sloshing rubber boots was her father's only way to pass the woods and his love of hunting onto his children. She recognized her position in the group-- guest and tolerated tag- along. Marty was her father's closest friend; he had three sons and a baby daughter who would never go hunting or take part in the male rituals of forest secrets and story-telling. Her father took some joking from his friends about dressing a girl in wool pants and handing her a gun to carry through the woods. Women's liberation and the sexual revolution made few real changes in the minds and attitudes of the men who prowled the Adirondack Mountains in the 1970's; to them, escaping women was a main reason to go into the woods. But her father really seemed to want her there, and would not give into her mother's complaints about the language, the drinking. Over time, Jill became a source of pride for him. A better shot than any of the boys her age, quite a few of his friends lost money betting against her at the hunting club picnic when she shot twenty for twenty, striking each target, dead center, in under five minutes. And just last fall, he let her take aim in the duck blind at the flowing punctuation marks in the sky. Two fell; black objects growing bird-shaped as they splashed into the flat, bottomless October water. She couldn't wait to be old enough to dress in camouflage, color her face with the greens and grays of the woods and sit watch on Blind Man's boulder or work a drive, stalking the deer through crunching leaves and early frost. Eventually she planned to kill a buck with the big-scoped rifle, then pose for a picture kneeling beside her prize.

"Jill, I'm going out," he yelled from the bottom of the stairs while she put away her laundry, and she grabbed her coat and jumped in the cab of Marty's truck without even asking where they were going. She was happy to be there until the details of the hunt started to become clear; her driving lesson would allow them to stand in the back of the pick-up and fire away at rabbits. Still in their winter fur and the snow gone in a wave of warm air and rain that hung the breath of spring over everything, the animals sat amongst the dead leaves, piled brush and other winter refuse, believing themselves as camouflaged as they had been several days before.

"They think they're safe as virgins in church, huddled up under them bushes." Looking where Marty pointed, Jill counted five white spots, obvious as the heart of a target, not fifty yards off the track, and her stomach grew tight. With her father and Marty in the back, cruising along in the unexpected sunshine of this January thaw, a slaughter was imminent.

"Let's get to it," her father said, rubbing his hands to-

123

gether. "Ready to drive?" Marty stopped the truck and before Jill could answer, they both opened their doors and hopped out. Her hands sweating on the wheel, she listened for the first shots, but heard only scuffling as they settled into the truck bed. Her father had shown her how to move from park to drive. "All you'll need. And for God's sake don't gun it." She looked to see if he was joking, but he was gazing out toward the weeds and low bushes that grew up the embankment and carried on until the real woods began.

He shook his head as he stared, "Almost too easy." But then he gave her a quick pat on the shoulder. "You'll be fine. Brake on the left, use it when we knock. Otherwise, foot just barely on the gas." He reached behind her and flipped the latch on the sliding rear window. "Yell if you need me."

Marty's first shot exploded just as her father shut the driver's door. The truck shifted with his weight when he went over the right side to retrieve his prize. Then the quiet tap above her head and she moved the truck out of park. There was a certain level of fear, her body small behind the truck's wheel, as she got it plodding along the bumpy ties, right wheel hugging close to the dull metal of the abandoned track. At the speed they traveled, though, there was little to do and it soon felt familiar.

Her thoughts turned to the hunt that wasn't really hunting. She recalled her father's voice on afternoons in the basement, serious as he cleaned the guns, their stocks quickly gleaming like newly washed hair. He possessed an endless litany of rules: "Remove the bullets after each drive, carry the gun in the woods with the chamber open, never point any gun, not even an unloaded one, at a person, shoot to kill or save the bullet." His hands along the barrel and stock were certain, strong, and she watched carefully. Some days he guided her hands through the motion of the cloth along the barrel, but either way, his lectures and stories kept on in his measured voice, a sacred connotation, engraved on her brain like stone prayers. He built a monument to hunting in her mind that this January day did not match.

She could just reach the gas and brake pedal by straining forward with her right hip, which she did each time the quiet thud sounded on the truck roof. This hollow noise was distinct from the clang of beer cans emptying from the cooler and piling in the truck bed as she drove. After each stop she clenched her shoulders, hugging the wheel until the pistol blast echoed off the bank of trees and she felt the lurch of the pickup bed as one of the men jumped over the side to retrieve the kill. Then an entirely different bump of a noise as Marty or her father lobbed the dead body of a rabbit. This was the empty knock of a carcass, dead flesh unmeasured, insignificant as Halloween pumpkins kicked from the porch at midnight.

Down the tracks they continued, a percussion section leading them through the pattern of drive, drink, stop, shoot, retrieve. In the winter woods where the empty branches clacked their secret codes, Jill sensed doubt like the faint sour at the mouth of a milk carton; she refused to look at the bleeding white pile mounting on the truck bed behind her. Sometimes she couldn't look away from the cowering, shaking mass just before it shuddered and exploded; nose twitching, ears pressed flat on a shaking head, it looked like a small child on the school yard surrounded by taunting classmates. Eyes wild, shifting side to side, it crouched. When her father and Marty missed, she could smell fear, a rank and underground heaviness that mixed with the smoke from the gun barrels. Even then the foolish animals could not forego instinct and run. Every quivering inch made visible the impulse for flight, but they remained, uncamouflaged in the dead underbrush.

"My goddamn feet are soaked," she heard Marty say as he landed in the truck bed.

"Jill'll go for some." Her father offered; his voice as matter of fact as if he were lending a chainsaw or stepladder. She put the truck in drive with a quickly mumbled prayer, "No more, please no more." But minutes later the soft roof tap and the blasting of the gun, this time off the passenger side.

"Got your boots on right?" Her father asked. Jill considered a refusal, but what argument was there? Her father brought her to the woods; her father told her to do this, and even though her skin writhed with goose flesh at the thought of the shattered body on the ground, she would obey.

Outside the truck cab she had to squint in the bright

sun as she looked up at her dad and Marty scanning the tree line just off the tracks. They shielded their eyes and held their pistols with one hand, their beers with another. She could see the stretched, stained whiteness of her father's t-shirt where his black and red hunting jacket flapped open. Finally, he looked down at her and raised his chin in the direction he wanted her to go. It was the same directional cue he used for their Labrador, Noodles, from the side of a duck blind. No words, just a language of eyes and gestures that guaranteed obedience.

"Hold up," Marty said just as Jill forced her body off the side of the truck. "There's another one." After much bending, pointing and confirming, Marty said, "Go head, I've got the most so far."

"Against the truck," her father commanded as he sighted in. She pressed into the contoured metal, wishing to meld with the pickup's door, wishing she was home, until the gun's crack split the air. In the bullet's echo came a loud, piercing squeal, like fingers on a chalkboard over and over to the rhythm of a rapid breath.

"What is it?" Jill asked, covering her ears.

"Winged him," she heard her father say. "Give his neck a crunch before you pick him up."

"But Dad, I can't. I don't..." Trailing off in disbelief she looked up at him, helpless and hoping, shrugging with her hands still covering her ears.

"Got you a sissy, huh?"

"Naw, she'll go." And his brown eyes looked into Jill's, flat and serious as the mud in which she stood. She knew the look from other times when she and her sister were playing loudly or behaving impolitely somewhere. The look was also familiar from another hunting trip when he sent Noodles out of the canoe after a duck and she refused to go. Marty had been there with some other men from work; their chuckling began when the dog sat still in the moments after her father's signal. Three times he ordered her over the side, rocking the canoe and waving until Jill clutched the gunwales in fear they would capsize. Quivering, her wet beaver tail between her legs, Noodles sat there until he finally picked her up and dumped her into the swamp. She retrieved the duck but would never go near the water with Jill's father again.

"Go on." He signaled again toward the shrieking noise, and she started away.

She stepped between puddles, trying to jump onto grass tufts wherever possible. Hands still pushed against her ears, she made slow, unbalanced progress. Along the edge of the tracks, dead grass and earth appeared solid, but gave way to icy water, still partly snow. Her boots filled with liquid. Each step was another chance to get soaked or fall, and then she would have to remove her hands from her ears where the noise was a nightmare from which she could not awake. The edge of the woods rose a few feet and then turned black with heavy shadows. She would have to go through some thin bushes and under a pine tree to her target, a writhing mass of white, twenty-five yards away. Until this final shot of her father's, Jill had never known a rabbit could make noise. Like deer they were silent, nervous animals, skirting the crowd; now the howl haunted her and she tested the air every few steps, hoping the noise would subside. But in pain and the last few moments of its life, the rabbit became a machine of sound, loud and terrifying as Jill moved closer.

She arrived at the edge of the forbidding pines, afraid of the dying animal, certain it would bite her if she got close. Fumbling through the brush, she tripped and landed face first among the bracken and poking sticks. Her hands fell from her ears, and the hysterical scream of the rabbit reverberated like a heavily struck gong. A branch poked her in the eye as she climbed back on her feet, and tears surfaced to mix on her cheeks with the mud from her fall. She stood at eye level with the lower arms of the pine tree. Into the black shadows of the tree she stepped, and the noise deafened her, rose to a shrill frenzy. She blinked and tried to focus in the dusky shade. There were still small patches of dirty snow beneath the tree, but the rabbit was not hard to pick out among them. It cleared a circle of earth around its collapsing body from kicking and frantic leg motions, tossing up the pine needles and dirt. The shot split the upper body apart into a bloody pile so it could not right itself to run; but its lower half did not seem to know this, for it spun in a near perfect circle of useless motion. Blood seeped into the ground making blackened patches, and the rabbit's spattered sides jerked and panted like a fish tossed on shore. Turned on its side, only one eye was visible, looking straight up as the body continued its rotation. Jill could see the dark pupil roll to the front and back again to be replaced by cornea. In the dark, sound-filled alcove she pulled in her breath and took a hesitant step closer. It scrambled, panted and scrambled a bit more, hunching a foot or so further from her. The legs continued their running motion, pushing at the earth, but they stopped for long moments and seemed to grow weaker. She took two quick final steps, closing the distance, and stood towering over the bloody mess of rabbit.

It was only medium-sized, about twice the length of Jill's foot. She knew precisely where to step to kill it, to end its squirming and screeching. There wasn't any scrambling away now; the legs barely moved, just an occasional spasmodic jerk, the sides heaving, its pupil still rolling in and out of sight. The eye could focus, tighten on her face for a second before it got swept away. She raised her foot; took aim at the curved area just below the head. If she planted her boot in the right spot, she could shift her weight and snap its neck, easy, painless, merciful. But she couldn't do it.

"One of the worst things a hunter can do is allow an animal to suffer." This rule of her father's, lectured and proclaimed, sounded in her head. There was nothing to fear, no danger to her and the misery would end. She had to do it. Leaning forward, ready to bring her foot down, the rabbit's eye rolled toward her again. One leg began the deep instinctive push to run, but flopped a few times and then shook. Her stomach churned and she cried harder. She just didn't have it in her. Sniffling, she began to back away and jumped when a hand landed on her shoulder.

Over the slowly dying squeal he said, "I got it."

He took his hand quickly from her, barely masking his disgust, and turned to the shuddering animal. Shame and anger, thick as melted wax, burned her insides. Her father was merciful. He belonged in the woods. She ran toward the truck, then slowed to a walk as the squealing, hissing cry snapped off. Her father's flattening steps came up behind her. He passed without a word. They were both in the truck when she got there. Her father stepped out to let her in, and Marty drove a few tenths of a mile to a dirt road crossing the tracks where he turned around. Jill watched the trees pass, a green pulse of color on either side of the truck and let the tears fall, refusing to wipe them as they slid down her cheeks and dropped onto fists she could not release.

On Her Feet

They were given the back bedroom, the only one with a double bed.

"I assume those are your arrangements," his mother sniffed, coldly liberal as she placed clean sheets in her son's arms.

"Only a few months. While we get on our feet," he told her, stroking her back while they finished a picnic by the lake near David's childhood home. A few early orange leaves drifted to the ground, their flames like blown out matches. Marcie had left college with a year to go, following David because he asked, following David because what if nobody else ever loved her like this; her heart too afraid to lose him, she put away school, for now.

It was a breathless, untended room, painted shut windows and a dark mahogany bureau hulking like a chaperone in the corner. His mother used the closet as storage for her summer clothes and they rested on ancient wire hangers, sweaty and useless at summer's end. An antique wooden bed filled most of the room's space, a bed from a time when people were shorter. David's body did not fit. The end board struck him at the ankle, leaving his feet to dangle in space and empty of blood each night while they slept.

Marcie propped pillows at the bed's end to form a more gradual slope, but David still woke each morning with tingling feet, white like the bellies of dead fish. Needles shot up his legs when he lowered them to the floor. Marcie rubbed them back to life before taking her shower. She knew how her hands on his feet delighted him; with his eyes closed he moaned and whispered "yes, yes" while she watched the clock's slow forward trickle. But the house impressed her; she loved to stand in the dining room and imagine herself serving dinner, moving around

130

the mahogany table with tender, hesitant caresses, stopping before the china cabinet, dustless and blinking its cache of crystal goblets.

In the evenings she began taking long walks under the emptying canopy of leaves, watching how the autumn clouds whisked over the hills like time lapse photography. She still wished to move that fast through time, past the stalled moment, the living in a place not her own. But now, when she thought of this long-awaited move with David, she felt sure he would refuse to fly there with her. On these walks she found herself turning up curling driveways, tree-lined and stone-pillared where they met the public road. Mansions, contemporaries, big, small, she loved each house she discovered, longed to walk with ownership through a front door, to turn into a driveway after dark and swing headlights through windows she washed. On the porch at David's parents, she would dry her tears, hurry upstairs to their short bed and try to forget the furniture and curtain designs filling her mind.

Most of the time his parents ignored their living arrangements by remaining silent, eating dinner without them and retreating to the noise of the television. But on Wednesdays they played bridge.

"This is our son David." Drawing him into a deep, triangular hug. "And his friend Marcie," they added to the Barretts, their bridge partners. "She's staying with the family for now."

"You're just being paranoid," David told her in their room a short time later.

"But they never speak to me. And you saw them just now. I'm staying with the family. I could be some poor, pregnant relative."

"That's not how they see you."

"They don't see me at all. Have you told them we're engaged?"

"When we can afford a ring, I'll tell them."

"They hope I'll go away. We have to get out of here. Get our own place."

"Here we go again. Why not rub it a little deeper in my face that I'm not selling insurance or writing grants in some

131

stupid office. Or maybe I should go sell overpriced jewelry with you?"

"I'm just saying if you had…"

"…a job. I know. You only say it a thousand times a week. I swear you pester more than Mom and Dad. How nuts is that? I wouldn't have brought you…" He turned from her then, the danger of his sentence like a heavy pendulum building momentum between them.

"What? Finish. Go on. You wish you hadn't brought me along, hadn't pulled me up from the gutter to live here. Say it."

"That's not it. Don't put words in my mouth."

"Then finish your own."

"No. This conversation is over." He left then, calmly as if they had been discussing what they needed at the store. It frightened her, the scalpel he could use to carve out emotion and throw it away. He would not be back to finish and would never speak to her on the topic again; she was alone to figure it out.

In late November, David's mother took him to a doctor for his feet. No permanent damage, but he was instructed not to sleep in the short bed anymore. He moved down the hall to his old room and the twin bed with the baseball sheets. Surrounded by the wallpaper of his childhood, he slept again near his parents, a thin shell of plaster separating them.

Coyote Moon

A woman I once worked with came to visit when I moved back east and stole my car after my husband and I went to bed. To be fair, it had been a rough day with her own vehicle dead in our driveway, her bank account empty and three bottles of wine gone between us when we should have been eating the lasagna I made.

She called me at 3 a.m. from the police station a county away. I couldn't imagine, fumbling in the dark for my phone, what could be wrong. In fact, when I recognized her voice, I wondered why she was calling from our guest room downstairs.

"It's the fucking coyote moon," she said. "Makes me do crazy shit."

Ten minutes later, in the cab of Rich's pick-up, I tried to explain what might have happened.

"Tell me again why I'm driving to the Massena jail in the middle of the night?"

The clouds were thin layers of bone dust, letting through the yellow light. I pointed.

"A coyote moon."

"That's her shit, not yours."

"Aren't you glad though?"

We didn't speak again as the miles rolled beneath his tires and frogs jumped in the road, their mighty back legs carrying them into the circle of a headlight as if they leapt in the center ring of a circus. Sometimes there was a thud as the bumper ended the performance. A few miles outside of town, swampy farmland shifted to forest and we continued through a tunnel of dark, the moon now only slatted light. Busy with the speed of pine trees out the window, I didn't see why Rich swerved and hit the brakes, his arm thrown across my chest as I slammed forward in my seat belt. One kick of a back hoof knocked against the hood as the deer somehow cleared the front of the truck.

I took his hand as he guided us off the road's shoulder and kissed each finger before placing it in my lap where I wanted its warmth to remain.

"Fucking safari out here," he said, his laugh shaky.

In the parking lot of the town hall and jail, I hopped out of the truck and noticed how many spaces were taken up by police cars. It didn't seem possible a town the size of Massena could have a dozen vehicles set to round up lawbreakers, but there they sat, white and empty beneath the parking lot lights. My Camry, the only other car I could see, sat alone and dark in its own row furthest from the entrance.

Rich lit a cigarette and walked around the front of the truck, checking for deer damage. Fluorescent light beamed at me from the glass front doors as I pulled one open. A woman in uniform sat behind the counter, her eyes on a computer screen. Somewhere in front of me, echoing off walls and the tile hallway, a voice full of fury and cursing violence reached my ears. I pointed, and the policewoman rolled her eyes and nodded. I imagined the shrapnel sound of Kate's cries had been unceasing.

"You fucking dyke. You think you rule this hick shit town. What a fucking joke." And the sound of metal crashing into metal. As I turned the corner, two uniformed men stood staring into a cell, their arms across their chests. It was her voice for sure, but who was she yelling at?

Beside the officers, their view becoming mine, I looked into the cell where Kate stood with her fists clenched at her side, her whole body like a small dog straining at the end of a leash. On the other side of the cell stood a woman in a dark robe, like a choir robe was my first thought, but then I realized, she was the judge. Tall and thin, her gray hair cut close to her head with a slight wave, her feet in flip flops and peeking out beneath the robe, a strip of white lace, she too stood with her arms crossed, a surprising sense of patience about her as she leaned against the wall. At her feet lay a metal tray surrounded by spilled food and what looked to be an upturned coffee cup. Kate was not wrong about the fucking coyote moon; something bad had happened and seemed to be still happening. I pointed in her direction, one of the officers shrugged, and I tried to remember if I had ever spoken directly to a judge. "Your highness," was all that came to my tired mind, but she turned toward me before I spoke.

"Are you responsible for our guest?" Her voice was not unfriendly, but like certain teachers I remembered from high school, a tone that made me want to avoid making her angry.

"I am your honor," gratitude for my mouth's ability to recall those words, even as I wondered if I would regret claiming Kate. Still standing in her fighting dog stance, she didn't even blink. The judge turned away from her and stepped to the door, pushed and was beside me with the cell closed in one smooth motion. There was a click as the door locked in place.

"I am Judge Dinova. And I would very much like this woman out of my town."

"I'll bet you would, you Nazi tyrant. Your town my ass." Kate's voice attacked the air. My jaw dropped, but I kept my eyes on Judge Dinova.

"You can see why I got out of bed? They cannot simply let her go," here she gestured toward the officers. "But I can if I'm satisfied she'll disappear."

"What did she do?" As soon as the words were out of my mouth, I regretted them. I didn't actually want to know or want this woman so clearly dragged from her bed in the middle of the night to think I was going to defend Kate. Rich was waiting in the truck, how I longed to back out of the hallway and pretend I didn't even know the raving woman behind the bars. How much did I owe her, this guest turned thief?

"The officers picked her up after she smashed into six mailboxes along Constant Boulevard and damaged lawns in the process. She refused a breathalyzer, but as you can see..." We turned together to look through the bars. Kate didn't appear to be listening; now she stared at the floor, all the tension in her body gone, like she deflated.

"Does she have a history of mental illness?"

"I don't believe so."

"How well do you know her?"

"We worked together in California. She just came to visit." On our back porch Kate told me about getting fired, the recent fight with her daughter who married a Naval Officer and moved to North Carolina, but wouldn't tell Kate her address, and the latest boyfriend who walked out of a Chinese restaurant before the egg rolls showed up. The thing about Kate was how funny she made all this sound. Tears rolled down my cheeks laughing as she imitated the waiter's reaction when she threw the white dishes and stormed out, leaving the wonton soup to drip down the wall. The mess never really touched her, at least it never seemed to. In the three years we worked together, such tales were fairly common, the world always a difficult place for her to navigate, but always surprise on her part when it tumbled down, some frustration and anger too. My co-workers all called her Crazy Kate, their voices like children on a playground when she wasn't there to defend herself. To her face, they were quieter, avoiding her tongue. I did not speak any of this to the judge.

"I should charge her." Judge Dinova's voice reached my ears in a stage whisper. "But then she would have to stay here." I nodded. If they didn't want her here in jail, what was I supposed to do with her?

"Is it your car with the New York plates? I nodded, again wondering if I should admit to so much. Would Rich say I should have asked for a lawyer? Was I somehow part of this crime through my car?

"Can you promise she will not cause any more trouble?"

"Some things have happened I think?" I was stalling, not sure I could take her out to the truck, take her home, take her anywhere at all.

"But can you promise?"

"She's supposed to stay a week." I waited to let that many nights of Kate create a clear image for us both. "I can try and convince her to cut it short."

"That would be ideal. Maybe by this afternoon?"

Five minutes later we were walking down the antiseptically bright hallway. The judge handed me my keyring, heavy with the good luck turtle Rich brought me from South Carolina; it had been in Kate's hand when they cuffed her. She stared at the floor and walked, my hand on her arm like she was an invalid or very old. I nodded at the officer behind the desk and held the door as Kate stepped into the dark. The door closed behind us, and she shook my arm away.

"This fucking place is incredible. Who could live in such a shithole, backwater, bullshit town? What the fuck are you doing here?"

I was still walking toward Rich's truck as she screamed at me; the sight of him like spring water as he eased himself off the bumper, ready, attentive, mine. We had only been married for eight months, but his eyes, tracking me as I came toward him, made we want to propose to him, marry him all over again.

"Let's get something straight," I said to Kate, ready now to handle her with Rich beside me. "You did a really fucked up thing. I don't know why, but you're lucky you aren't still sitting in there. So, shut up and get in my car, cause I'll leave you here if you don't."

I pointed toward the far side of the parking lot and glared straight into her eyes. It was entirely possible she would ignore me, keep raving, and I wasn't sure if I would really leave her, but I put every bit of anger I felt into my stare.

"The coyote moon does crazy shit to me too, so move it." And the funny thing was, she did. I worried the entire drive home that she would reach over and grab the wheel or try to jump out the door. Following the red glow of Rich's taillights, the miles ticked off.

"They tried to lock me up out there too."

"Maybe you need a chance to rest."

She didn't answer or even seem to hear me. Waves of energy, like a sunburn or radioactivity came off her as she perched on the passenger side of my car, her silence bigger than the sky I tried not to look at. The moon hung in its place, made of plaster it seemed in all its stillness. Kate never glanced at the light it spilled around us.

Kendall's Garage showed up and towed her car in the morning, replaced the belts that were making the engine overheat, and by lunchtime she was on the highway, pointed south, out of town, away from the small roots of a family I was tending. Rich and I sat on the porch at sunset; he pushed the metal

137

swing with a steady foot as we let the quiet, the fireflies, and the first shadows of bats emerge around us. By the time the moon rose over the full night sky, I could imagine Kate in another state, and we were inside watching TV.

Helpless

The family dog came home with a mouthful of newborn rabbits. Two intact, but bloody, a third its belly torn open, small pieces poking out. They were each a bit larger than a pack of gum. Casey was eleven and still believed damage could be repaired, broken things set back in place.

Her father put Duncan in the basement because she could not stop screaming at him. He pawed and whimpered at the door, but Casey refused to listen. She built a nest in a shoebox she dug out of her closet. An old T-shirt formed a soft base, which she covered with grass. As soon as she had them settled, she worried about the one with its body ripped open, the gray pieces like bits of dead worms. Her mother tried to tell her it could not be sewn back together, so she stomped from the table and got the needle and thread herself. But when she returned, her mother lit the match and held it to the needle's end for sterilizing; she rested her hand on Casey's shoulder as the metal heated to a glow.

There was no sound, just the slow contraction of their sides. A tiny paw, like a seed pearl, twitched on the largest of the three. The squeal of a dying rabbit, like the time Casey watched her grandfather's cat catch one in the garden, would have been welcome in the silence of slow breaths. She wanted them to fear her hand as it moved toward them in the box; instead, they remained still as she used her pinkie to poke the slick pieces back inside.

"This will have to do," her mother said, laying a toothpick on the table. Casey tried again, her hand shaking as the wooden end pushed at the organs, shifted and pushed, trying to fit all the impossibly small pieces back inside. She moved the needle to the rabbit's skin and held her breath as she felt it penetrate, a stitch to pull two sides back together as one, but it would not hold, ripping through the pink skin as she prepared for the

139

next one. When all of it came spilling out, her eyes blurred. Then the body went slack, like it emptied and hollowed when she touched it with the needle again. There was a deeper stillness, and her mother's hand was quick to cover hers.

"It's gone," she said.

Casey jumped from the table at her mother's words, kicked the dog dishes across the kitchen floor, and ran from the room.

On the big rock at the side of the yard she sat staring at the sun, her eyes squinting open so the hot spikes of color could fill her head. She could not see the flayed belly one more time, could not let herself picture Duncan's teeth piercing such softness.

"Your mom's heating sugar water." Her father hopped onto the rock beside her as he spoke.

"It died."

"I know."

"While I was trying to sew it together."

"I know."

"They're so little. So helpless." A breeze shifted across the field of grass as Casey spoke. She felt its chill shudder up her spine. "And Duncan attacked them. Why were they even alone?" The questions nearly split her open.

"It's what they do. Like the cat at Grandpa's."

"That one was eating the tomatoes, raiding the garden." How could she make him see the difference, the impossible moment the tiny body had been lost? She gagged with the picture once again in her mind.

"There's an eyedropper for the other two if you want. It might not work. They're awful small."

Together their gazes drifted across the field. No way to know how many more nests cowered beneath the grass, hidden but not safe.

"I don't think I can."

"We can throw the whole mess in the burn barrel and be done then." He jumped from the rock and began brushing off his jeans.

"Dad, no. We can't…"

140

"We can't just let them suffer."

She sighed, jumped down beside him, and readied herself. It was a truth she knew, a truth she would never be free from, a truth she could dislike but not ignore.

"Duncan's not sleeping in my room anymore," she said, as they walked together toward the house.

Baby of a Friend

There are no cars in Paula's driveway and this surprises me. I pictured aunts making tea and sturdy uncles or cousins standing about looking awkward, their presence a comforting barricade. On the floor of my van rests a carrot cake and a large stainless steel pan filled with lasagna, three cheeses, sausage, hamburger, tomatoes from my garden. I balance my way toward the porch with this offering. Early October rain falls in calm streaks of cold that paint the gravel driveway, the collapsed heads of lilies, my arms in their red windbreaker. I knock with my elbow, intentionally too quiet to hear. The thought of putting the food on the steps and racing to my car almost overpowers me. But then a crack of warm air and her eyes in the open slot.

"Paula I came as soon…" She has turned away and I talk to empty space. I push the door open and enter. Inside it looks like the bottom of a lake, a filtered, sifting dark. Not a light or an open window anywhere, and the floor has toys, clothes, empty shoes, piled like small anthills down the hall and into the living room. A quiet ticking rises to my ears and I look at my watch; its hand swishes away seconds while nothing else stirs. In the kitchen I place my pans on the counter, still stepping over the strange, planted piles. Everything else appears spotless, untouched, not a spoon or coffee cup or dishtowel to be seen. I have no idea where Paula is and it feels improper to stand in her kitchen while she hides somewhere in the house. But what is the right thing? What would I need someone to… I cannot simply leave, so I move back down the hallway and into the living room, my feet clunky in the delicate silence. She sits in front of the television, in a wooden rocker with tied-on cushions. The chair is only a few feet from the screen, but she does not face it.

"Where's Ed?" She creaks a bit and turns to me.

"I don't know." Wearing a bathrobe, shapeless as empty grocery bags, her body sinks in the chair. Her hands flutter out

142

from beneath her, caressing senseless space. A baby's bassinet sits in view, white, strangled lace haunting the room.

"Are you... Can I..." But her hands have grown still, all of her now hunched within the room's shadows, part of the shadows. Out the window I see orange maple leaves in the breeze, realize that the wind still blows, my car still sits in her driveway, the minutes on my watch still tick away. In a few months snow will cover the ground and she will have to face Christmas. I begin to shake then, to feel the tears opening, my mouth gagging on a moan. Nothing in the room seems to notice me leave, and I am halfway home before I think of January, the 15th, not so long after Christmas. Noah would have been one.

I call my mother from the road. "Complications from the flu."

"Nobody really dies of the flu."

"Don't you watch the news?"

"Not someone we know."

"Didn't Nana's father die of the flu?" She only sighs, but I can hear the tears in her throat. "Well I just dropped food at the house and she... He died of something."

"Can you and Bob come for dinner Sunday?" I almost press this conversation back to her, punctuate the moment with the grief I need to taste. But my son is her only grandchild.

"I'll check and see."

Lucky at Cards

I was nine when Grandpa threw a kitchen chair at Grandma during my Saturday visit. When she ducked, glass from the china cabinet shattered, while he stormed off in a wave of curses proclaimed in at least three languages. She moved me to the living room while she swept up the mess of twinkling fragments and told me stories of her childhood in Canada, how she skated for hours on a pond clear as the bathroom mirror, shining back the sky like a Christmas carol. Hours later, she dealt cards for rummy with a bandaged hand, while I listened for Grandpa's van in the driveway, my ears tuned like high powered antennae.

As we lay down our hearts in runs to the king, she argued all the reasons to avoid marriage, keep my own life and never let a man take anything from me. I reminded her, "you wouldn't have dad if you didn't get married and without dad, no me." Three aces down for the win, she looked at me, her face still and serious. "You don't miss what you never had."

Virgin Prayers

The Holy Virgin Mary, exact replica of the statue from the entryway of St. Theresa's Catholic School, appeared in Jesse's shower one Tuesday morning. About three feet tall, she gestured with her small hands for him to move closer. Her sapphire robes swayed in the corner, solid against the white tile, but the water did not reach her. He covered himself before screaming, "What the fuck?" Then regretted his words as a tear, blue as marbled earth, slipped down her cheek and she looked at the ground, away from him, ashamed for him.

Hail Mary full of grace ... the words came to his mind unbidden as he crouched in the steamy water and tried to hide his nakedness. There was every reason to believe the vision was a hangover remnant, too much tequila, no doubt. But the words of the prayer continued, the Lord is with us. He turned away from the corner and water sprayed him, stinging his eyes, slicing at his cheeks and lips like small knives.

"You need to take better care of yourself, Jesse." The voice was a confusing mix of his grandmother and Miss O'Hanlon his fourth grade teacher, the only one who was not a nun that year; she had been young enough to smile often, and she wore her long curls in a ponytail that Jesse imagined whisking across his face. She smelled of vanilla and the heat of summer when it radiated off beach sand; thoughts of her made him swell and redden with shame as her red pen made check marks across his math worksheets.

Blinking away the water, he looked again in the corner and the Holy Mother stared back, her hands out toward him in supplication. Ignoring the shampoo still in his hair, he shut off the water and wrapped himself in a towel. From outside the shower, he looked back and saw nothing. What did "better care" mean exactly? He chewed on the phrase throughout the day, whenever he couldn't push the incident away from his mind.

The next morning she reached up and slapped his ass while he soaped his hair. He screamed again, whirling around and expecting to see the girl he just left in his bed, Amy, Amber, something like that. "You must take better care of others, Jesse." He noted the idea of a theme and saw also how she scowled a bit, her voice a little rougher, less Miss O'Hanlon and more his grandmother after she'd had a few. She stood with fists in the ready position. *Blessed art though among women and blessed is the fruit of thy womb Jesus.* The prayer again an echo in his brain as he shut off the water and tried to forget the sting of her hand branding his cheek.

For two days he showered at the gym after work. By Saturday morning he was ready to brave his bathroom again, so he stood beneath the water, waiting. He tried to pretend he didn't know what this apparition meant when she scolded him, tried to believe as he closed his eyes that "better care" might mean waiting for their orgasm. He used condoms; everyone had fun. What was her deal?

She did not surprise him this time. But the look on her face had gone from stern and intent to furious. Her lips as she cursed him, spit out the words, "I warned you Jesse." He faced her, unafraid and ready. No shower vision was going to ruin his twenties or even make him feel guilty. With his hands on his hips and his junk on full display, he prepared to answer back. *Holy Mary, Mother of God.*

"What do you fucking want? Is this some burning bush kind of thing?"

She shook her head, downcast eyes again, a moment benign and sacred, mother of Christ in a patient, long suffering froth of blue robe. *Pray for us sinners, now.* Her eyes lifted to him as the words of the prayer, like footsteps down an empty hallway echoed in his head. *And at the hour of our death.* In her hand, the razor he kept on top of the soap. *Amen.*

Pomegranate Sin

In fourth grade, Stacey Spafford brought a pomegranate to school, trapped in clear plastic. I watched this jewel beneath her desk, poked at its staining weight during spelling. Mrs. O'Hanlon never caught us, turned away writing the list of loops and whorls we would be expected to repeat on Friday like penitents. Stacey had not written the words, but asked me for them at recess, still clutching the bloody fruit, her ticket to the day's attention. She wore a blue dress, too small across the chest and missing three buttons, a hole where her skin bulged through. I thought of my mother, what she would say of Stacey if I tried to explain the dress and the pomegranate. "Stacey Spafford has the kind of mother who buys ridiculous food and ignores life's essentials."

And I would nod in agreement, wishing, even though I knew it was a sin, that I had a mother like Stacey's.

"Can I have the words or not?" I stared at the meaty center, its spiraled garnet filling her hands. The wet pulp pressed against the bag like a packaged heart.

"I'll give you seeds. That's what you eat." It hushed me-this knowledge.

Who decided such things? I opened my palm; she counted out four. At my nose, the smell of candy apples as teeth crack their autumn shell-sweet and sour at once. I squeezed them in wonder. Should I pop all four in my mouth? How hard should I bite? Stacey watched while I struggled with the need to have their taste. Before I could bring myself to ask, they pushed through my fingers, squirting and landed in the dust at the base of the silver slide, coated in a dirt batter and useless as rocks.

"Can I have another?" She laughed, "forget it, don't even need those stupid words," and twirled away in her too small dress while I tried to hold back my tears.

The Meat Counter at Kingsley's Market

I saw my first dead bodies the summer I turned twelve. I spent those hot days of July with my neighbors, Adam and Susan, perched in front of Kingsley's Market, a stoop with steps on two sides, a pole in the middle, so you had to choose left or right as you climbed the steps. From the left side, we had a view down Market Street as far as the railroad tracks; from the right side, a view of the gravel parking lot that ran the length of the store all the way back to the loading dock. We watched this side the most since our aim was the candy truck that came twice a week, delivering, we hoped, a new supply of Charlie's Angels Trading Cards, the fad and passion of our 1977 hearts. Old Mr. Kingsley, who ran the front of the store, came out regularly to chase us away, a swearing scarecrow of a man, scattering us on the wings of our laughter for as long as it took the dust to settle back into the gravel. If he was threatening enough or the day hot enough, we might jump on our bikes to check Sholette's Grocery downtown, even though their candy delivery came later, or head off to the town beach to swim, skip rocks, and let the lifeguard yell at us for a while. But mostly, we hung out on Kingsley's stoop.

Old Kingsley's son, Robbie, not much older than us and a Vietnam vet, had been running the meat counter at the back of the store since his discharge. When I was young, I stood in front of the counter, staring through the glass at slabs of cold cuts while my mom ordered chicken or asked to see a particular roast. But that summer, I didn't go to the store with my mom, and on the hottest days, Robbie whistled to us from the loading dock and slipped us cold Yoo-hoo or Pepsi, smiling while his dog tags bounced gently against his blood-stained butcher's apron. He winked at me that last July day, passing the sweating bottle of soda into my hand, and I turned away blushing. After he disappeared into the dark of the store, I pictured him slicing bologna and grinding the burger our moms would serve for dinner, then driving his Mustang to my house, honking for me to come out. His smile made him look a little like the men chasing after the Angels on TV and walking them along the beach in the sunset.

Back on the stoop, we drank our sodas, still waiting for the truck that had not shown up, discussing the likelihood of cards that day because Monday had been a bust. I was four short of a full set; when flipped over, these cards made a jigsaw puzzle of the Angels in silhouette, just like the credits on the TV show. I needed three stickers, two of Sabrina and one of Jill. My neighbor, Susan, had two of the stickers I needed but wouldn't trade, unless I gave her something to get her closer than me to the finish. We had an unspoken race underway, both of us dedicating our allowance and any money we could gather from extra chores or rooting around in the couch cushions. Packs were a quarter each, and I planned to buy twelve if the truck ever arrived. Susan's brother Adam was not far behind us with his collection, although he didn't usually put all his money into cards. I don't know how much Adam cared about the Angels, but Susan and I loved everything about them, their feathery hair, their wide-legged pants, how they could run in high heels and still look beautiful. They were grown up in all the ways we weren't, all the ways we wanted to be.

When Adam was with us, we threw rocks while we waited, dialing in some pretty fair aim for hitting the stop sign at the top of Flint Avenue, where it came to a T with Park Street and made the border of Kingsley's parking lot. The noise when we hit the sign was usually what brought Old Kingsley out to holler at us, even though we were smart enough not to throw any when there was traffic. Winslow was the kind of town with mostly empty streets, where you could make a game out of holding your breath between cars and lose most summer afternoons. Since we didn't want him chasing us away, we held back on the rocks, hoping we could wait in peace. When the time seemed endless and the truck a fading dream, Adam grabbed a handful of stones off the driveway at his feet and began picking out the bits too small to throw.

Just as he tested the first one in his hand and stood up to ready himself, a pick-up screeched around the far end of Flint and fishtailed on the gravel as it twisted to a stop. We knew Gary LaDue's truck, had seen it parked by the town barn plenty of days when he was off as part of the town crew, cleaning bridges or stopping traffic for the endless potholes they filled all summer, only to have them freeze and buckle again each spring. I had also seen him on the 4th of July, at the block party held each year in the park downtown. He danced under the lights in a set of spins all his own, then rushed at the drummer and tripped over some cymbals. After the crash and a pause while everyone stared, he stumbled, away from the band, then flanked and held upright by his wife on one side and his father on the other.

But as he jumped from his truck that afternoon, he was alone and not stumbling. We watched him reach above the seat to his gun rack, like the one in almost every truck in town. He slammed the door and moved at a trot away from the stoop toward the back of the building, climbing the cement steps of the loading dock two at a time, a shotgun in his hands. In 1977 it was not unusual to see a man grab his gun as he left his truck. I watched my own dad carry his Remington into fields, along streams where we fished, into the house after work. So, it took a few seconds for us to realize he was running into the store, fast, with a gun in his hand. Adam jumped up first, nudging me.

"Let's check it out." And soon all three of us started toward the steps Gary had just climbed.

The first shot came before we reached the top of the loading dock. Together we ducked and crawled up the last two stairs. I could see in through the open door, only strips of clear plastic in front of me, as I looked into the dark corridor toward the store's back end. The white metal edge and glass front of the meat counter were in view. Another shot rang, and we heard a loud thump like a bale of hay falling off a truck. For those first moments, it was just an adventure, the tension of a TV show, like I was one of the Angels edging around a parked car or creeping up on the bad guy, ready to karate chop a gun from his hand. Then a voice started screaming, and Adam kept creeping toward the swinging strips of plastic. In the spaces between the loud screams, I heard the whir of the coolers that ran along the back wall of the store, how odd those two noises were together as the familiar sweating glass doors came to mind. Without thinking, I followed Adam inside, more curious than afraid.

We knew the shotgun only held two shots in its dark, chambered heart; we wanted to see what those shots were about, so we stepped quietly through the plastic and into the light of the dairy aisle. Old Mr. Kingsley stood with his arms in the air near the shelves of canned vegetables, while he screamed at Gary, not words, just long wailing. Gary never looked at him, just stood on some boxes piled in front of the meat counter, gun still raised. And that counter, glass as always, but somehow it looked like meat had been thrown up and against the back surface, a glistening, shiny covering. Beside me, Susan turned away, and I heard her puke, just as I realized it was blood, Robbie's blood now plastered red and slick on the back glass.

"You can't squirm away you bastard." A click and Gary threw the shotgun to the floor. A noise of crawling and then a clatter as something fell to the ground behind the counter. Old Kingsley stopped screaming when the gun hit the ground. He dove toward it as Gary pulled a pistol from the back pocket of his jeans.

"No dog tags gonna save you. You think you can take my wife? Take anything you want cause of Nam?"

Gary cocked the pistol as he said this, and another shot echoed through the store. Adam jumped and scrambled behind me.

"Come on, Mary." His voice hissed at me, but I swatted it away. It was my chance to be an Angel, unstoppable, brave. I had to watch whatever was happening. He and Susan ran away down the aisle, but I stayed, watching Mr. Kingsley, his mouth moving and silent, until he too moved out of sight. Gary never took his eyes from his target, cocking another time, his only focus the world behind the counter. *Six.* I whispered the number; there were six in the heart of this small gun. The blast came again. I could see him, high on his toes as he aimed over the counter. I stayed still, peeking around the corner, my body flat on the floor, my eyes frantic as I waited.

"That's for Mindy," he screamed from his perch on the boxes. Not a sound came from the space where Robbie should have been. It was only a second, I may have blinked in the moment when Gary's rage shifted, and he put the gun to his own head. A third deafening blast and he fell to the dusty floor, his face now level with mine and the rack of potato chips behind him spattered with his blood. It all lay before me, impossible to unsee. Where moments before there had been so much desperation, now on Gary's face, in Gary's hand, throughout Gary's body, emptiness. A siren in the distance, its soft throbbing call grew stronger as I got to my knees and then stood, shaking and still feeling the echo of gunshots, in my ears, but also in my chest, in my head, like a gong struck and still quivering.

It would have been smart then to walk toward the front of the store, to join my friends somewhere outside where the world hadn't been shot to pieces. But Robbie just winked at me, a few moments before, two lifetimes ago. I pictured him pulling into my driveway. Now I stepped toward the horrible scene at the meat counter, couldn't walk away until I saw what was left of him. I edged carefully around the small ponds of blood spreading across the floor where Gary had fallen. Almost nothing remained of the left side of his head, but I didn't look for long since it made my stomach lurch. I climbed on the boxes still in place, needing to see Robbie.

I felt the heavy, thick residue of gun powder and death as they latched onto my skin, filled my nose, guided me. I was connected to Robbie, his wink, the cold bottle, his smile like a quick promise. He knew us, thought of us on those summer afternoons when he worked his job and we sat outside in the dust. The nightly news showed the world what Vietnam looked like, what confusing jungles and atrocities my parents said our country stumbled into.

Robbie survived, been set free, sent home to restart his life. I had no idea if he had done something to Gary's wife; I knew what those things might be for sure, but no way of guessing if there was some kind of justice repaid. But still I climbed boxes, looked at the mess on the floor, a roughly human shape, a cavern of red where his back should have been, now linked always to the meat behind the counter.

This was a scene never facing the Angels. Guns fired, cars driving away, the police showed up, the music shifted, and they got their man, handcuffed and safe. Nothing awash in blood, mangled or unmoving when they returned to the office to await Charlie's call. Hands grabbed me and carried me out the front door. I didn't resist. Officer Foster placed me on the fender of the fire truck, wrapped a blanket around me; I matched Susan and Adam. It was hot in the sun, but we held them around us anyway and nobody spoke. I looked at the ground, looked at the parking lot filling up with neighbors, tried to stop seeing the back of Kingsley's store.

"Murder suicide." The phrase mumbled through the crowd outside, an electric prayer prodding more and more people to show up in the gravel parking lot to watch. For years to come this phrase would stick behind my closed eyes like rugged, blood-soaked letters, a mystery Charlie's Angels would never solve. Their trading cards, so important that morning, faded away, forgotten in our drawers and empty shoe boxes before the first leaves of fall crisped and fell. The cards actually died for me that day, outside Kingsley's, watching the town surge toward the store and the shock of such a summer afternoon while Mindy, Gary's wife, ran toward the store, screaming with a baby in her arms and her long hair flying out behind her. Two officers held her back, their hands pressing her between them, trying to turn her away. Despite all the gossip and small-town whispering of that afternoon and beyond, I never knew for sure which man she screamed for.

Ten Thousand Things

"I'd love to get out of the house for a bit," my grandmother told me, her shoes already tied. My mom stood by the door and shrugged in my direction. We came to visit because I was only in town with my kids for three days and Grandpa was dying. It had been a fact since October when my daughter was born and the oncologists spoke, but now, early July, he was too weak to drive or spend time out of the house. Hospice was the next step, but not quite yet, so they got along with my parents stopping by each day and Grandma getting out when she could.

I settled Colin on the carpet with a handful of matchbox cars and lifted Emma from the car seat.

"Bring her to me." Grandpa took off the oxygen mask he had been wearing and smoothed the plaid blanket sitting across his lap. He wore one of his work shirts, a soft green chambray we had given him for Christmas, two pockets for his pipe and tobacco. But it hung on him now, the cuffs with inches of empty space around his emaciated wrists, each bone on his hands looking carved and prominent without flesh to soften it. He didn't seem strong enough to hold her.

"She won't sit still," I said, kneeling as I set her down beside his chair. "I'll put her close. Watch how she pulls up." His eyes followed Emma as she swung her chubby legs into crawling position. I stayed beside him on my knees.

"Boy," he called to Colin as Emma reached the pile of toy cars. I tapped Colin on the shoulder to let him know Gee-Gee was speaking to him. "That cane in the corner and the music box. Bring them."

He pointed across the room where a varnished wood cane with a gold tip and horse head top rested against a china cabinet. Every bit of was loaded with the furniture and glassware they would not get rid of when they sold their larger home for a duplex in town where it would be easier for Grandma to get around. It was the only time he acknowledged how sick he was.

The room smelled of too many breaths without open windows, the slow decay of Grandpa's illness as he coughed up thick black mucous and the Clorox wipes Grandma used on every surface. Colin moved toward the cane, a caution in his step I had never seen before.

"This one?" He sounded much older than his four years.

Grandpa tried to answer, but the coughing started, and he grabbed a wad of tissues to cover his mouth.

"Just bring them," I said and waved him back to us, hoping Grandpa's cough would ease. With measured steps he carried the items, this boy who normally raced and tripped through the moments of his day.

"Here GeeGee." He stood close, but not touching Grandpa's recliner, the cane resting on the ground, the music box which was really a snow globe with white swans suspended above the surface of a mirror, held against his thigh as he waited.

"You hold onto this," Grandpa said at last, gripping the head of the cane and standing it upright. "It means more than money." He let it clatter to the floor then, and Colin jumped at the noise. The snow globe shifted and fell toward the ground, but Colin scooped it back into his hands and offered it to Grandpa. The room held its breath, the three of us staring and waiting. Then Emma crawled back toward me, her body gliding over the end of the cane and onto my lap where she began sucking her fingers and pulling at my hair.

"I'm having more goddamn fun than you," Grandpa said, shaking his head. I wasn't sure which of us he meant, but hugged Emma closer as she relaxed against me. He took the snow globe and turned it over like it was a delicate egg or small bird, showing Colin the brass mechanism that got the music going. It played "Sunshine on my Shoulders." My knees ached, but I didn't move. Colin took the globe with the glittering, fake snow falling on the miniature swans and sat down by crisscrossing his legs and dropping to the carpet, never taking his eyes from the slow drift behind the glass. With his hands on both sides of the globe, he shook again and leaned to show Emma, but she was almost asleep on my lap.

"I can think of ten thousand things to do with these two," Grandpa said. He stared straight into my eyes, and I could feel his rage like razors slicing into skin. "Ten thousand." And he pounded a fist against the arm of his chair. He groped on the floor without looking and lifted the cane. Holding it like a javelin, he cocked his arm and launched it across the room.

"Son of a bitch," he screamed as it wobbled in the air and cracked against the window less than ten feet away. The shatter of glass that should have been was not. Colin was on the move while I sat still in shock.

"It's ok GeeGee. Try again," he said, handing the cane over, his smile gentle with encouragement. "Mama says some things take time."

He threw it three more times, finally breaking the window, achieving success. As he sat looking satisfied, drumming his fingers with the music box's tune, I cleaned up glass, taped cardboard over the hole, and called the landlord. Grandma was furious at us both when she got home, even when I told her about the ten thousand things. She couldn't understand me when I tried to explain how angry he was and how Colin tried to help. Shaking her head at me, she went to make tea, unwilling to picture those desperate throws, how much he wanted to change something, anything around him. I did not mention the ten thousand things, how I now understood that he didn't have ten thousand of anything left.

Circus Heart

What is left most days is my grandmother's memory of the circus train. In the story she is young, with hair in two long braids, swinging like the curry-combed tails of horses. As she tells me her story, she ties these ribbons again to the ends of space where such memories lie. In that movement only, she could be a young girl, still new. And the crash, when it plays through, makes her shudder in her wheelchair where the nurse assistants move her in the morning after lifting her on and off the toilet and helping her put on clothes.

"I think she was about ten," my dad tells me when I go in search of crash details she cannot provide. "There was a picture on the front page of the paper."

The whole town ran the half mile to the tracks and arrived to find a dying lion, caged beneath collapsed train car walls. Wheezing as the light blinked to dark in his dusky, sky-filled eyes, he lost his jungle soul.

"His life just floated off, like a puff of cigarette smoke," she tells me one day when I find her still in her pajamas at noon. The nursing home staff cannot make her work in physical therapy, cannot force her to use the joints and tendons that have carried her all the miles of her life. When she refuses their exercises and encouragement, they wheel her back to her room where she sits, waiting for an hour when her body will forget how old it has grown. Each visit she remembers how yellow the lion's teeth were and the yapping of tiny dogs, the kind that wear collars and small hats in the ring, doing back flips and leaping through fiery hoops.

"I was supposed to understand something from that giant, dying head," she says. "I reached through and touched him, the fur just above his nose. There's a newspaper article with my picture. What did that give me? He felt like velvet, but what did

157

that mean?"

She fills out these details and wonders her questions again and again in the stall of these morphine days, surprising me by calling my name, making sure I am listening. Her fingers finally too weak to push for pain meds, the nurses stop taking her out of bed and ask me to hit the button while I sit.

"You can't give her too much," they insist. "It's set up that way.

Bats

My husband is a fine, impeccably dressed man, a pharmacist with curls like a baby and eyes looking through wire rim glasses with such firm purpose and belief in his own ability to control the world that I sometimes expect him to run for the senate or become a preacher. For a year after our baby died of SIDS, he brought home flowers every night, a rose the perfect red of angel's blood, a vase of tulips, a basket of carnations and mums. Five nights a week of flowers, as if trying to convince me through the sheer volume of flora and fauna that the world was still a beautiful place. I smiled for him, hugged the glorious porcelain of his bones cast in gray and black Armani suits. But each morning when his car left the driveway, I made the rounds of the house, gathering every stem and petal and carrying them to the basement where they spent the day, until a few minutes before he was due home. I could not be alone in the rooms of our house with all those bits of colorful life. How could he not remember the endless baskets around the toy chest-sized coffin? They felt like cruel jokes those flowers, but I knew he only wanted to help me heal, make me ready to give my heart away to a new baby. I could not explain the crumpled, empty state of my heart, any more than I could explain the flowers, and so I was pregnant again, before our daughter Marcie would have been two.

Soon I touch the skin of my sleeping son, cool where the residue of clammy fever has broken at last. With the fans and air conditioners rattling like highway traffic, I have to place my hand on his chest, smaller than a baseball mitt, and then briefly across his mouth to feel, for sure, his breathing, gentle as puppy tongues. My husband will soon come to bed, after tightening us in the house with his system of locks and alarms intricate as a dancer's routine. I will be nearly asleep when he climbs in beside me, our house a fortress, linked to the police, the fire

159

station, the ambulance. I will only mumble with my face turned away when he tells me "the place is secure."

But instead, his wild face in the doorway, a tennis racket in each hand.

"Get the baby; there's a bat," and he is gone; his feet quickly sound the stairs. I follow.

What're you doing? Get Timmy." But I stand in the filtered light and search the air for our dark intruder. When it flies at me, I shriek and cover myself reflexively from its halting swoops and cuts. Paul swings, but misses in the middle of his own recoil.

"Dark beast," I mutter, and he glares at me, waves me away. I see how useless we both are beneath its unpredictable angles, attacking and large.

"Go on!" Frantic now, he yells as it circles in desperation, an insistent, angry geometry of flight. "Shut the door and stay with him."

I read a book once about a woman who lived near bats and allowed them to swoop around her, diving for their meals of insects, while she sat peacefully beside a tree and drank freshly pressed cider. Unlike her, I am terrified almost to paralysis, crying now as shadow wings curse the air around my head. The stairs are nearby, and I am quickly on the second floor, slamming the door of Timmy's room, scooping him sound asleep into my arms, for I must push away those diving wings. In our house, somehow this symbol of darkest evil has made its way through secret holes and tunneling nooks we never knew were there. There could be hundreds, waiting, growing, arriving when we let down our guard.

I touch my fingers to Timmy's mouth, search for the delicate cup of air he exhales, a slight tickle across my skin as he sucks in his next breath. Through the dark comes muffled banging and a few tiny vibrations as Paul's stomping hunt shakes the floor. He is a good husband and father; he will kill this bat no matter how long it takes him. But sitting in the stillness of Timmy's room, near the crib that was never Marcie's because I insisted we buy a new one, I can feel the texture of the future and its promised ordeals. It has a smell, this waiting, like a trunk of rotting fur coats and animal pelts forgotten in the corner of some attic. It will be there always, will win through the depth of its patience.

Now Timmy's hair, small patches of fluff on the heat of his scalp, so perfectly round. And there is the horror, the full wash of losing him alive in my body, drowning me in an ache fathoms deeper than my bones, until I nearly throw him from me, want to take back the part of me he has already claimed. I cannot go through it again. There is no passage out of losing a second child; so I wish him gone. My choice, my terms, an end to waiting for the worst to happen. I want to live without the fear of his death, to wake once in bed without ears and heart leaping out to search the night for his noises. And I feel my hand at his breath, his lips, crushing…nearly. His head thrashes, once, twice; one foot flies out and strikes me under the rib. I release us. Shaken and afraid, I hold him at arm's length despite his whimpers. Rock the chair to my heart's frantic beat, and whisper, "I'm sorry" as fast as I can.

He quiets and I draw him back, arrange him in the crook of my arm with uncertain balance and wait. The silence beneath me stretches to a minute, two minutes and then the crack of yellow as Paul opens the door. He must see my tears like small diamonds, for he kneels quickly by my side and strokes them away with the gentle caress of his thumbs.

"It's gone, it's gone," he coos, then touching the baby, "It's OK. How's my little Timmy?" I let him stand me up, feel the slight release as he draws our defenseless son from my arms and lays him in the crib.

"Come to bed. We're safe now." But hours later, beneath blankets in the cave of our warmth, I lie, awake and frozen in the knowledge of all I must hide from my husband who protects us.

Risking a Goddess

We met on the beach during a full moon. Six of us, swollen with children, weighted with worry, exhausted by the effort of hope. Carrying armloads of tulips bright as baby toys we gathered on the sand. It had begun as a joke, a whim to call forth Hecate, goddess of midwives, from her place behind the moon. We needed her, for we had worries; the ugliness of life on the planet seemed to percolate around us now that we walked with children in our bellies—our steps more careful, our path more cluttered. The future became a field of land mines, and we were frightened. So, we joked about witches, mother earth, goddesses with the power of change, in the minutes after childbirth class, in the moments before la maze while our husbands and partners fetched cranberry juice and bottles of cold water. During breaks, when the bathroom was full, six of us in a line whispered the names of all the forces we knew. Somehow the conversations became a plan while our men rubbed our backs and we learned to puff in the ways of labor. Who knows how these things happen in that mysterious third trimester, the uncertain world of the spirit? But we ended up on the beach, at night and we made our plea; we knew somehow to find a crossroad, someone knew to search out land and water and sky and place ourselves at their meeting. We knew to make a circle, to join hands and leave the men at home, unknowing.

We knew to call her name three times and listen for the barking of thirteen black dogs. When the dogs encircled us, snapping with angry teeth, we chanted through the fear.

Tears and wild eyes as we began to beg, "Hecate please," "Hecate, please," "Hecate, please," until the dogs ran into the ocean and turned to silver fish arcing high over the surf like rainbows of the night. A ladder of twinkling rope fell

162

from the moon, and we all gasped a bit when she appeared in the light, bent and covered in a burlap robe. Down she climbed, swaying in and out of our sight, until she reached the sand and moved toward us with a pail, then passed out cookies of plump raisins and melted chocolate. The pail was raised to each of our lips, pouring out a river of icy milk. Never speaking a word, she gathered up the crumbs we dropped and carried her pail back to the ladder.

"Hecate, thank you. Hecate, thank you. Hecate, thank you." We knew to be polite. But really, we weren't satisfied, not yet safe until someone called, "Can't you wait?"
"We have questions," said another. "We need your help," I yelled, feeling my swollen belly twist with life.

She turned back toward us then, her face crooked with anger, "You cannot give them more." Her voice came from the sand, from the sky, from the water. "Would you take the living world from them with your fears? Who are you to be untouched by the chances of life?" She looked round the circle and we felt sudden rocks where hearts had just beat, where pulse had just spoken. She held each of us there, our bodies suddenly caskets for the babies we carried. When at last she began to climb the ladder, her voice, clouded and dark said, "Did you pay attention?" And merciful life refilled our wombs. We dropped to the sand, sobbing as the wind picked up to sail her back behind the moon. In rhythm with the waves as the tide crept toward us, we rocked on the beach until morning.

ACKNOWLEDGEMENTS

For as long as I can remember, I have wanted to see a collection of my fiction in print. I am beyond thrilled and grateful for *A Drawn and Papered Heart* to be making this dream come true. Any project of this size has many people to thank.

I'll begin with my family: Jim, Sam, and Claire for all the ways you accept my scribbling and the hours I shut myself away to work. Thank you and know how much I appreciate your love and understanding.

For Tony Burnett, Mary Day Long, and all the staff at Kallisto Gaia Press, thank you for making this a better book than it was and for the time and effort you gave to make it a real object in the world.

Thank you to all the anthologies and literary journals, print and on-line, where many of these stories first appeared: *Story, The Baltimore Review, Mid-American Review, New Delta Review, The Potomac Review, Gargoyle, Amazing Graces: Anthology of D.C. Area Women Fiction Writers, Smokelong Quarterly, Apple Valley Review, Eastern Iowa Review, Split Lip Magazine, Chagrin River Review, Mad Cap Review, Fine Linen, Backbone Literary Journal, Twin Cities Review, Foliate Oak Literary Magazine, Tallow Eider Quarterly, Dying Dahlia Review, Peacock Journal, A Lonely Riot Magazine, River and South, Sky Island Journal, Light and Dark, Coal Hill Review, Lily Poetry Review, Red Coyote, Ocotillo Review, Furious Gravity: Anthology of D.C. Area Women Fiction Writers, South 85 Journal, Flash Fiction Magazine, Allium Literary Magazine,, Works Progress,* and *On Her Feet.* Without these bright spots of acceptance and publication, I am sure I would have struggled to keep believing in these stories and their potential.

For support and belief in me as writer, a few editors and writers in the DMV have been especially helpful. I want them to know how much I appreciate their help: Richard Peabody, Susan Muaddi Darraj, Melissa Scholes Young, and Moira Egan. Thanks to Kathy Fish and Nancy Stohlman for great workshops and amazing advice. And thanks to the Writer's Center in Bethesda where some of these stories found their form.

To my sister, Linda Konkoski, for her stunning cover art and all the conversations about creativity and its place in our lives. Thanks also to John Burger for the help with the cover design. You and Linda make a great team. To my mom, Bonnie, for giving me books as a kid and letting me read whatever I wanted. To my dad, Bruce, even though you aren't with us any longer, your mark is on this book in many ways. To Jane and Anne, sisters and friends, so many of these stories have places, small roots, and bits of our shared lives.

To all my students and colleagues in the high schools I have called home: Marian Catholic, Lisbon Central School, Chesapeake High School, and Broad Run High School. Thank you for being part of my teaching days. I have been lucky to talk about books and writing all day with wonderful teenagers and those who teach them. Teaching is as much a part of me as writing; I am grateful for our time together.

Thank you to future readers of this book; please keep searching for books that engage you, for voices that matter, and for the small presses and bookstores that make them available.

Printed in the USA
CPSIA information can be obtained
at www.ICGtesting.com
JSHW020502180324
59338JS00005B/167